Hue

"Are you awake?" Sage whispered

Jackson lay sprawled in his backyard hammock, one arm shading his eyes. From under his arm he muttered, "No, go away. I'm dreaming about you."

"Isn't the real me better than a dream?" she murmured suggestively.

He moved his arm to peer at her. "Why do you ask?"

"I have a plan." Sage grabbed one side of the hammock and heaved it up to one side. As the hammock swung violently and Jackson toppled out, he snatched her by the waist to pull her with him. They landed in a heap with Sage on top, straddling his hips. Every inch of him was as hard and sexy as any man she'd ever dreamed about.

"Not another plan." Jackson gave a long-suffering sigh. "Does it involve moving?"

"In a certain sense." And then Sage began running her hands over his bare chest, boldly stroking lower....

Carla Neggers was certainly busy during the publication process of *Family Matters*, which features the sister of the heroine in her previous Temptation, *Trade Secrets*. Carla gave birth to her second child, a boy, and moved from Massachusetts to Connecticut—then back again. But even through all the upheaval, this witty storyteller managed to come up smiling *and* meeting her deadlines. Now that she's settled, we're urging Carla to pen another rollicking Temptation for her readers.

Books by Carla Neggers

CLAIM THE CROWN

HARLEQUIN TEMPTATION
108–CAPTIVATED
162–TRADE SECRETS

Family Matters

CARLA NEGGERS

Harlequin Books

TORONTO • NEW YORK • LONDON
AMSTERDAM • PARIS • SYDNEY • HAMBURG
STOCKHOLM • ATHENS • TOKYO • MILAN

Published February 1988

ISBN 0-373-25290-0

URGENT!! URGENT!! URGENT!! URGENT!!

TO: SAGE KILLIBREW
    MOUNTAINBROOK SKI LODGE
    ASPEN, COLORADO

SAGE: NEED YOUR HELP. NOWHERE ELSE TO TURN. BRING FORTY THOUSAND DOLLARS IN HUNDREDS IN PLAIN BLACK BRIEFCASE TO THE HAPPY TRAILS HOTEL IN SAN DIEGO THIS FRIDAY. BE IN BAR AT 9:00 P.M. WILL SEE YOU THERE. REPEAT: URGENT.

GRANDPA KILLIBREW

1

THE HAPPY TRAILS HOTEL wasn't one of San Diego's finest, and as Sage Killibrew made her way to a dark corner table in the lounge, she wondered if her grandfather normally frequented such places. Had he become a drunk? One of the legion of homeless? With Grandpa Killibrew anything was possible. As she sat on a rickety chair, Sage placed the plain black briefcase on the floor between her ankles and wondered, not for the first time, if she was out of her mind.

A waitress in a short, flouncy dress took her order for a glass of white wine and a glass of ice water. Looking askance at the woman's outfit, Sage told herself she wouldn't be caught dead in a dress with a bodice down to here and a hem up to there. She didn't even wear stuff that skimpy to bed! For one thing, she was of an athletic rather than a curvaceous build. For another, she'd freeze. Since she'd hoped against hope that the Happy Trails wouldn't be the kind of place it was, her own attire for the evening was a departure from her usual simple, straightforward clothing: a striking white suit with a peplum jacket, silver earrings, stockings, heels. She was five foot nine, blue-eyed and strong, and her tawny hair was as long and wild as any Killibrew's had ever been. She could swing an axe, climb the Rockies, ski any slope in Colorado and survive weeks in the wilderness with difficult teenagers. But shoes with heels over an inch and a half defeated her.

Not, however, her waitress. *Her* heels were at least four inches.

Sage whipped out an old black-and-white photograph that showed Grandpa Killibrew standing on a dock in Maine with the wind in his hair and the devil in his eye. "Excuse me," she said to the waitress, "have you by any chance seen this man? He'd be about twenty years older now."

The waitress leaned over, coming perilously close to popping out of her bodice. Sage wondered if this was how Grandpa Killibrew liked his women. She hoped not but realized she couldn't possibly know. She hadn't seen him for twenty years.

Bodice intact, the waitress shook her head of curls. "Nope, not that I know of, but I see a lot of men around here. Don't remember most."

Sage nodded and tucked the photograph back in her jacket pocket. She'd expected as much. The Happy Trails was located on the outskirts of the barrio and seemed safe enough, if tacky, but the clientele wasn't all that memorable. At just before nine on an October Thursday evening only a dozen or so people—men, she should say— were gathered at the bar. A basketball game was on the gigantic television screen. Sage was the only woman being served as opposed to serving. She wasn't one to feel uneasy just because she was outnumbered by the opposite sex, and if push came to shove, she figured she could handle anyone who got out of line. But she doubted she'd have to: no one had given her so much as a second glance. It was the suit, she decided.

It wasn't that she expected trouble, or had even taken Grandpa Killibrew's telegram seriously. She'd come to San Diego and the Happy Trails a day early to check things out—to reconnoiter, she'd told herself. So far, however, she hadn't seen a sign of her long-lost grandfather.

Her wine arrived, cheap house wine, she was sure. She leaned back in her chair and relaxed, turning her imagination loose as she looked around the dim, seedy bar. The swinging half doors were in the style of an Old West saloon, and she could just see them bursting open, with some gunslinging desperado sauntering in. He would have to be tall. Taller than average, say, six foot four. And dark, preferably with black hair and black eyes. Blue eyes just wouldn't do it. Too tame. And, of course, he would be broad-shouldered and slim through the hips, so his holster would slide down just a little.

And he'd have a scar. Sage smiled to herself. He'd have to have a scar. It would be on his face somewhere, not disfiguring, just menacing. He wouldn't smile and he wouldn't laugh and he wouldn't drink white wine.

It'd be whiskey. Straight.

Every woman in the place would swoon—except for her. Nope, she thought, no way. She'd had her fill of sexy cads and desperadoes and such. Old Auntie Killibrew insisted Killibrew women were destined to fall for rogues, but Auntie's rogues were all romanticized, not real. They were all kind and wonderful underneath their tough exterior. But not the ones Sage had dealt with. They'd been tough on the outside and tough on the inside, and they thought kindness and sensitivity were for wimps, although Sage viewed such traits as signs of strength. But she'd learned: if a man had the devil in his eye, he probably had it in his heart, too.

Feeling relaxed, Sage fished an ice cube from her water glass and popped it into her mouth. Helped kill the taste of the cheap wine. Seedy as the place was, she hoped Grandpa Killibrew was here. He was wild and eccentric and irresponsible, but Sage, more than any other member of the unconventional Killibrew clan, was the one who had most regretted the disappearance of the man who had founded, and then bailed out of, Killibrew Traders, the family catalog clothing business. That he hadn't "disappeared" but simply upped and left after the death of his wife in the mid-1960s didn't faze Sage. The Killibrews all had that urge to do something unusual, different. Quite simply, she'd missed him.

The swinging doors suddenly crashed open. Sage jumped slightly and looked up—and nearly choked on her ice cube.

Her man stood there. He was tall, dark, broad-shouldered and slim through the hips. From her table in the corner she couldn't tell if his eyes were black or if he had a scar. He wore a khaki bush shirt and faded jeans, but no holster.

He stared silently, menacingly, into the gloomy lounge. Sage wasn't sure whether she wanted him to notice her or not.

Then he sauntered up to the bar and ordered a whiskey, neat. His voice was very deep and he didn't waste words. Sage watched as he turned his back to the bar, and she felt her heart begin to pound when his eyes fell on her. He didn't smile. Taking his whiskey, he walked over to her table and, without waiting to be invited, sat down.

He had a small jagged scar on his right temple, and his eyes weren't black but a deep, deep violet, the color as unexpected as the eyes were impenetrable, and hardly tame. Sage's mouth went dry. Perhaps she should have booby-trapped her briefcase, she thought vaguely. Then, if the wrong person opened it, kabam. But such extreme precautions had seemed, well, absurd. As absurd as

Grandpa's telegram. Forty thousand dollars in a brief-case. Good God! But here she was, and there was the black briefcase, which she'd bought specially for the occasion, on the floor between her feet. Today, however, was Thursday. Even Grandpa didn't expect her tonight. The man across the table—a figment of her imagination though he might have been a moment ago—couldn't have anything to do with her grandfather or his bizarre telegram. Probably just a good ol' boy making the moves on her. She could handle him.

"Evening," he said.

There was nothing of the good ol' boy in his low, steady voice or the startling eyes that gazed at her with such frankness and interest. He was a good-looking devil, but Sage knew better than to let her guard down.

"Evening," she said, mimicking him as she drank some of her wine. "I'm drinking alone."

He raised his glass. "No one should have to drink alone." Still not smiling, he downed his whiskey in a couple of swallows and set the empty glass down on the table. "It's not a good habit to get into."

Sage felt herself tensing, ready to do battle with this man. Her sister, Juniper, just married to a handsome rogue of a man named Calvin Gilliam, was the consummate businesswoman and would have remained cool and distant. But Sage wasn't like her sister. Cool and distant wasn't her style; hotheaded and direct was. She'd chased off bears and mountain lions. Why not a tall, violet-eyed man?

"That's my business," she replied, heat coming into her voice.

"I suppose it is. Did you just get in?"

What made him think so? Just that she didn't look like a typical Happy Trails customer, she supposed. He was really distracting her now. She wanted to be keeping watch for Grandpa Killibrew, not looking into this man's all-too-tempting eyes. In the soft glow of the cheap candle on the table they were unreadable. She couldn't even guess what he was up to.

"No," she said, "I didn't, and if you don't mind—"

The waitress brought another whiskey for the intruder, who hadn't even ordered one. It was that way with some people, Sage thought, turning down a refill. Her plan of action had called for an evening of reconnoitering, not dealing with strange men who'd materialized from the depths of her imagination.

"I assume you flew in from Colorado," he said.

She couldn't keep an expression of surprise from her face as her head jerked up and she studied the man across from her with renewed interest—and a sudden, clinical objectivity. He knew she was from Colorado, but how? Had he found out somehow from Grandpa? Her heart began to pound. Good God, was he really in trouble? She hadn't believed so, not for a second. When she'd received his telegram, she'd just figured that, being a Killibrew, he wanted to make a dramatic reentry into the lives of his family. Or maybe he just needed the money, but not for anything, well, not for anything that would involve a man like this. Violet-eyed, unknown to her and strangely compelling. Grandpa couldn't possibly have anything to do with this quietly self-possessed individual.

Fine, Sage, but how the devil do you know?

It was true. She had been seven when her grandfather had made his exit, and now she was the first to hear from him. She didn't know who he could be involved with, even who he was. Her grandfather. What did that mean? He could be a scoundrel playing on his granddaughter's childhood memories, her fondness for him, for financial gain. He could be using her.

She wished she'd ordered that second drink. "What makes you think I'm from Colorado?"

His expression remained placid, controlled, but his unusual eyes fell from hers, scanning and assessing what was revealed of her above the tabletop. Sage found herself growing warm in an unwilling, unpredictable physical response. She had to admit the man had a magnetic sexuality that was impossible to ignore, although she'd hoped she wouldn't respond quite in this way. She'd thought herself beyond all that.

He brought those haunting eyes back up to hers and gave her a half smile that made her hunt for any unmelted ice in her remaining water. There wasn't any. "Maybe it's your athletic good looks."

Sage sputtered, incensed. What a bold rascal he was! But not unobservant. She had always thought of herself as athletic, although not especially beautiful. How could she be when everyone told her she was the spitting image of Grandpa Killibrew? She had his blue eyes, although hers were round and wide, not beady; his wild, tawny hair; his stubborn, square jaw. Fortunately, she didn't have his bushy eyebrows and hairy chest. He wasn't a handsome man, but Grandpa Killibrew had always had presence—and that, too, Sage had inherited.

She glared across the table. "All right, just who the hell are you?"

The half smile almost broadened into a full smile, but not a very pleasant one. It was the sort of smile that conjured up images of old Auntie Killibrew and her rogues. Good-looking and sexy and dangerous as hell. This one had all those qualities, but Sage knew enough about herself and about *real* rogues not to be hoodwinked. Not this time. Not again. Never.

"My name's Jackson Kirk," he told her. The smile vanished. "And you're Sage Killibrew."

"Well, well, well."

He worked on his whiskey while she sat thinking, pressing her heels against the black briefcase. For some reason she wasn't surprised. Of course it would come to this. A seedy San Diego bar, a mysterious man who knew too much, a briefcase full of money. Sage felt like a character in a bad movie. The name Jackson Kirk meant nothing to her. Was it supposed to? Did he know Grandpa? Did he know about the telegram, about the money? Sage frowned. She was the only female customer in the bar. She must have been easy enough to pick out...*but* Jackson Kirk first had to know she'd be there. And no one did, not even Grandpa—she was a day early.

She smiled suddenly. Of course! "You asked about me at the front desk, didn't you? You peeked in here and spotted me and they gave you my name and where I was from. This'd be the sort of place to do something like that."

"No, I didn't have to. I'm a friend of your grandfather's. He told me you'd be here."

"Are you serious?"

"Very."

He certainly looked it, but Sage remained skeptical. "Where's my grandfather now?"

"He asked me not to say." Jackson Kirk spoke in that same low, steady voice. He might have been lying or telling the truth; she couldn't tell. "He found out you'd be here tonight and talked me into coming by to get the briefcase."

No! "I don't believe you."

"Why not?"

"Why should I?" She seized her almost empty glass and drained the last of the mediocre wine. Seeing this, the waitress appeared with another. Sage hardly noticed. This couldn't be happening! Jackson Kirk, whoever he was, wanted the briefcase and apparently expected her to believe everything he said and just turn it over to him. Did he think she was a moron? "Do you have any proof you're a friend of my grandfather's?"

"No, but—"

"Then I have no intention of giving you the briefcase."

His eyes narrowed, and they might as well have been black for the effect they had on her. This was a man who liked to have his way. Apparently he hadn't expected any trouble from Sage, which was his mistake. He said coldly, "I think you're being unreasonable."

"And I don't give a damn what you think."

Moving quickly, she jumped to her feet and snatched up her untouched, unasked for glass of wine. This was no time for subtleties. As Jackson Kirk pushed back his chair, looking every bit as menacing as the desperado she'd imagined, Sage didn't think. She simply acted, impulsively throwing the entire contents of her glass into his face. Then she grabbed the briefcase and ran.

Behind her she heard a distinct "*Hell!*" It wasn't steady, and it wasn't controlled.

And it didn't stop her. The men at the bar had turned to see what all the commotion was about and were looking in confusion from Jackson Kirk to Sage. As she raced toward the swinging doors, Sage yelled to them, "Please don't let that horrible man follow me." Horrible man? How corny, she thought, but for added effect she added, "*Please!*"

They started in a pack toward the violet-eyed man with the scar. His eyes caught hers, just for an instant, but long enough for her to see the mix of emotions on his entirely too memorable face. He was furious . . . and intrigued. She had done the unexpected. Presented a challenge to him. *Surprised* him.

She wasn't sure she liked that.

Slowly he wiped his wet face with a napkin, his gaze never leaving her, seeming to promise her she hadn't seen the last of him.

Presumably, Sage thought, he was also wishing he had packed a gun on those lean hips of his.

BY THE TIME Sage had returned to her room and ordered up a late dinner of tacos and refried beans—something to glue her insides back together—Sage was finding more and more to worry about. She loved adventures, but here she was in a seedy San Diego hotel with a desperado type after her briefcase filled with money. Did he *know* there was money in it? Surely he did—or guessed as much.

And her grandfather, she thought with a heavy sigh. He was lurking about somewhere, too. God only knew what he'd been up to during the past twenty years. "Robbing banks, for all you know," she muttered, fiddling with the knobs on the television. She needed some distraction. But the television, of course, didn't work.

She flopped down on the spongy bed. What if the telegram had been a ruse? What if Grandpa Killibrew hadn't sent it and wasn't within five thousand miles of San Diego, California? What if she, Sage Killibrew, was being used?

It was an annoying thought.

Her tacos arrived. Nearly burning her insides as she consumed them, she pondered her situation. Could this

Jackson Kirk character have sent the telegram? Could he be the one who wanted the forty thousand dollars?

But how? Why? She didn't know any Jackson Kirk!

Maybe Grandpa Killibrew did. . . .

Oh, Lord, she thought, why couldn't the telegram have been sent to her sister, Juniper? But that was obvious enough. Even when Juniper was eleven—the last time Grandpa had seen her—she'd been the sensible one in the family. Grandpa must have known Juniper wouldn't have been able to help. She had the company, her husband, the Victorian house they were renovating. She wouldn't leave any of it to fly off to San Diego to help an ornery old man who hadn't had the courtesy in two decades to so much as send his offspring a postcard. Juniper just wasn't like that.

But Sage was. She was impulsive and always ready for an adventure and usually didn't ask questions until it was too late. Grandpa must have known the only Killibrew crazy enough to pay him any mind was his younger granddaughter.

Which meant, didn't it, that he had to have sent the telegram?

"Not necessarily." Sage scooped up some filling that had dribbled from her taco. Grandpa could just as easily have told someone else she was the granddaughter he could count on in a pinch. Or it just could have been a coincidence. "Either way, Killibrew, all you can do is stay out of trouble until tomorrow night and pray Grandpa shows."

Of course that wasn't all she could do, and she knew it. She could pack and head back to Colorado with her briefcase and what remained of her good sense.

And for the rest of her life she'd be haunted by questions and wonder if Grandpa had indeed shown up Friday night at nine, as he'd promised in his telegram. She had to face this problem head-on and get to the bottom of the mystery.

Her telephone rang, startling her. She stared at it as though she'd never seen or heard one before. Who could it be? Probably not Grandpa.

She picked up the receiver. "Yes?"

"Don't hang up, Sage."

Jackson Kirk. His voice was instantly recognizable, deep and sensual, his tone somewhere between a plea and a command. Sage clutched the receiver, feeling herself inexorably drawn to him. A dangerous feeling. "What do you want?"

"I'd like to come up to your room and talk."

She let her incredulous laugh be her answer.

It had no effect. "Your grandfather is getting himself into serious trouble. He's asked me to help, to bring him the money."

"What money?" she asked, eyeing the briefcase on the wobbly nightstand.

"The money in the black briefcase you had tucked between your feet."

Blast the man, did he know everything? "I don't have any money in my briefcase. I'm in San Diego on business."

It was Jackson Kirk's turn to laugh. "Not much skiing in San Diego, Sage."

She didn't like the way he used her first name, she didn't like his tone and she didn't like that he obviously knew so much about her. "Where's my grandfather?"

"I'll explain everything in person."

"You can explain everything on the phone!"

"No. I think we should talk face-to-face."

She hesitated. Jackson Kirk could very well be the only lead she had to her grandfather, but she didn't for a second trust his black-lashed, deep violet eyes. She shuddered, but not with fear, when she thought of them. She couldn't possibly have him up to her room. Not a chance. She was impulsive and daring, but not foolhardy. "All right," she said finally. "I'll meet you in the lounge in fifteen minutes. You can explain there."

"I don't think—"

"It's the best you're going to get, Kirk."

She heard him bite back something—a sigh, a grunt, a curse—and knew he wasn't pleased with her ultimatum. Good. She liked having some control over the situation. "Fifteen minutes," he said.

There was a click in her ear. When she replaced the receiver, she noticed her hands were cold and clammy, but she didn't let her uneasiness stop her. She had to move fast and think fast. She quickly dumped her lumpy pillow out of its case, at the same time grabbing the briefcase. The money was stacked in packs of one-thousands, neatly bound. Feeling like Jesse James, she shoved the packs into the pillowcase and knotted it. Then she ran into the bathroom and got a couple of hand towels, which she folded and shoved into the briefcase for weight.

Convincing, she thought. She supposed she should put the pillowcase in the hotel safe, but she didn't dare since Kirk could be skulking about the halls. And if he saw her, that would be that. Off he'd go with the money. Only she knew that she wouldn't lose anywhere near forty thousand dollars, but she did loathe being manipulated or outwitted.

There was nothing to do now but cross her fingers and pray that *she* could do the manipulating and outwitting. She stuck the pillowcase beside the other pillow on the bed and threw the spread over them. Not wanting to appear frazzled, she dabbed some raspberry lip gloss on her mouth and ran her fingers through her hair, her standard beauty treatment. Because of her outdoor life she usually had plenty of color in her face, and her eyes were so big and round and blue they rarely needed highlighting.

She decided she looked rather calm and collected, given the circumstances. Just before opening the door, she forced herself to stand still and breathe rhythmically for sixty seconds. Then, briefcase tucked under her arm, she went out into the hall, pausing to casually slip the Do Not Disturb sign over her doorknob. She didn't want an overeager chambermaid messing with her "pillow." Not that that was a real danger in this sort of place—she had yet to see *any* chambermaid.

There, she thought. One hurdle cleared.

Now it was onto the next.

JACKSON KIRK WAS waiting at the table where they'd sat earlier, another whiskey in front of him. As she walked across the dimly lit lounge, slackening her pace, Sage noticed how the candlelight flickered on his face, softening the features, and she saw not simply determination there but intelligence, too, and perhaps even sensitivity.

Don't start, she warned herself. *You're just imagining things you want to see. Obviously the man has certain undeniable physical attractions. That doesn't, however, mean he's intelligent or sensitive—something you, of all people, should know.*

She slid onto the seat opposite him. "Mr. Kirk."

He gave her that unreadable half smile again. "Sage."

After ordering coffee she noticed that the front of his shirt was damp and a faint odor of wine wafted about him. A direct hit. Under different circumstances, perhaps with a different man, she might have felt awkward or even embarrassed, but now she didn't. She felt inordinately pleased with herself, which bolstered her confidence. Scar or no scar, Jackson Kirk wasn't going to menace *her*.

"Planning to scald me this time?" he asked dryly.

She realized he was referring to the steaming coffee, which had just arrived. "Only if you ask for it," she said. "Now, Mr. Kirk. Talk. Tell me how you know my grandfather, where he is, what kind of trouble he's in and how my briefcase is supposed to help. I want facts and I want answers."

He gave her a look full of steel and maybe even surprise, and she wanted to grin. He'd underestimated her. That was a good sign. She sipped her coffee, which tasted as if it had been made about the time Grandpa Killibrew had departed the streets of Portsmouth, New Hampshire.

Kirk lifted his whiskey glass. "You're not what I expected."

"What my grandfather led you to expect, you mean?"

"Mmm."

"Well, what did you expect? Hair ribbons and my two front teeth missing? I haven't seen my grandfather for twenty years. He *did* tell you that, didn't he?"

Kirk took a hefty gulp of whiskey and slammed his glass down. "Hellfire." Any hint of sensitivity vanished as his eyes narrowed ominously, but he didn't raise his voice or seem anything but very calm and very much in control of himself. "You're not going to be easy, are you?"

"Not my style."

"I shouldn't think so."

She shrugged, and her eyes rested on his scar. She wondered how he'd gotten it, how he'd come by that air of quiet confidence. It was a quality she admired. So many of the men she knew were such show-offs. A sign of insecurity, she'd always figured. There was nothing insecure about Jackson Kirk, and that was something she found interesting and disturbingly provocative, if not heartening. A little uncertainty might have added to her own sense of confidence.

"I'm not here to talk about me. I want to see my grandfather. Where is he?"

"I can't tell you," Kirk said flatly. "I doubt he's even in San Diego. He told me about the telegram and asked me to pick up the money for him. Said you'd cooperate, you were a good kid. I was expecting someone...shorter and sweeter, I suppose."

She had to laugh. In all her life she'd never had a prayer of being short *or* sweet. "I'm a Killibrew, Kirk."

He nodded. "I should have remembered."

"Why does my grandfather need money?"

"He hasn't told me."

"But you think he's in trouble?"

"Yes."

Sage leaned back in her chair and drank some of the coffee as she appraised the man across the table. He could just as easily be lying as telling the truth. If he was lying, there wasn't much she could do except walk away and chalk this one up to experience: never trust Grandpa Killibrew and mysterious telegrams requesting forty thousand dollars. On the other hand, if he wasn't lying... Well, that, of course, was the problem. It left her with two basic, unavoidable questions. One, whether or not to believe him. Two, what to do if she did believe him.

"How long have you known my grandfather?" she asked.

"Not that long."

"A year? Two? Five?"

"About six months."

"*Six months!* And he's trusting you with forty thousand dollars?"

The words were out before she could stop herself, and she watched as two thick black eyebrows shot up and the scar seemed to whiten slightly. The violet eyes bored through her. "*Forty* thousand?" His voice was low and deadly. "You came all the way from Colorado with forty thousand dollars in cash? Hell, you're as damned crazy as your grandfather! You two deserve each other. Why I'm even bothering . . ." He broke off with a sharp curse.

Kirk's surprise seemed genuine. So he didn't know the amount Grandpa had requested and thus couldn't have sent the telegram himself. Therefore it *must* have come from her grandfather. That was something at least, Sage thought. Maybe this wasn't the wild-goose chase and great big mistake she'd begun to fear it was.

Ignoring his outburst, she asked, "How did you get mixed up with my grandfather in the first place, Jackson?" She used his first name judiciously, with the same casualness as he'd used hers. She hoped it would make him think her guard was down, that she'd decided to trust him, which, of course, wasn't true. "It couldn't have been easy."

But Kirk had regained his composure and answered vaguely, "It's a long story."

"I have time."

"I'm afraid I don't." He finished his whiskey. "I know you're confused and I know I promised to explain, but you'll have to trust me. Please, Sage. I'll see to it your grandfather gets the money, and I'll do everything I can to keep him out of trouble. I'll even try to get him to call you and explain."

"That's it?"

"It's the best I can offer."

She shook her head. "Not good enough, Kirk."

"It'll have to be." He held out one hand toward her, his expression stony. "The briefcase, Sage."

Since it only contained two hotel towels, she wasn't worried about losing it, but she knew if she didn't put up a fight, Kirk would get suspicious. Rearing back indignantly, she slammed down her coffee cup. "You're not serious!"

"I am." He didn't raise his voice. "You won't get away this time, Sage. If you'll look around, you'll see a man at the door. He works for me. At the bar are two more of my men. They have orders not to hurt you, but also not to let you leave this bar with the briefcase." He gave her a smile filled with confidence and an undisguised, raw sexuality that left her breathless. He knew the effect he had on her. "Not that I'll need them. I have a feeling I can handle you all by myself."

And I you, Kirk. But she tried her best not to look cocky. "Damn you."

"As you wish."

She rose with an angry toss of her head and gave the briefcase a hard kick. It skidded under the table and banged into his shins. Then, without a word, she spun around and walked away.

Her heart was thumping painfully when she reached the lobby, but she also had an unreasonable urge to laugh. She wished she could see his face when he discovered he had a couple of threadbare hand towels instead of forty thousand dollars!

Of course, when he did, he'd come after her. There was no question of that.

So she'd just have to be ready for him.

2

SAGE PASSED a fitful night with her bag of money as a pillow and had breakfast in her room—lukewarm coffee and a dried-out corn muffin. It wasn't an auspicious beginning to a day that already promised to be troublesome. During her countless bouts of tossing and turning she'd reasoned that her most promising course of action would be simply to get through the day, be in the bar at nine as directed in the telegram and hope Grandpa Killibrew showed up. *Without* Jackson Kirk.

Of course, the "simply to get through the day" part presented its own dilemma. She had visions of finding the violet-eyed stranger stretched out in front of her door or lurking in the lobby—or waiting to pounce when she emerged on the street. She tried to be blasé about it. After all, the most she could do was be on the lookout for him.

At least, she thought with a dry smile, he was easy to spot.

She put on her "expedition" jumper with its multiplicity of pockets, a soft chambray shirt and sturdy shoes. The white suit was banished to a heap on her closet floor. She was herself now. For a little pizzazz she tied a bright scarf around her neck. It wasn't that she anticipated meeting anyone she wanted to dazzle, except maybe a gorilla. She'd decided to spend the day at the renowned San Diego Zoo.

She thought again of Jackson Kirk. She was dressed for dealing with animals, and he was a dangerous beast. She would have to warn Grandpa about him, provided he didn't know already. That had been another middle-of-the-night decision: Kirk was no friend of her grandfather's.

A shiver ran up her spine, making her feel just like a heroine in one of the novels she liked to read on cold, dark winter evenings alone in the mountains. What if Grandpa didn't show up tonight? What if he couldn't? What if none of this had anything to do with him?

But it had to. Sage herself had only passed through San Diego once or twice, had spent virtually no time there and didn't know a soul there who might have passed her name and background to Jackson Kirk. That, of course, didn't account for Grandpa himself. There was no telling whom he knew and didn't know.

"To the zoo, Killibrew," she told herself stoutly and headed out.

She tried to make herself invisible as she tiptoed through the lobby, but there were few people about—it was relatively early, and this wasn't the sort of establishment where the clientele was up and about even remotely early. Including Jackson Kirk, it appeared. Nevertheless, Sage didn't relax until she was in a taxi on the way to the zoo.

It was a bright, clear, warm day, the kind meant to be spent outdoors. The line at the huge, immaculate zoo was long but efficiently handled, and soon she was off alone with her map, thoroughly entranced. Billed as the world's greatest, the zoo was as picturesque and as wonderful as she'd always hoped. For a while she was able to lose herself in the scenery, the birds, the animals, the sheer beauty of the day.

Shortly before lunch she stopped to view the tigers. Almost immediately a shadow fell over her. She didn't turn at once. She felt an unwelcome presence, though no sense of alarm. If she failed to pay attention to whoever was hovering behind her, maybe he'd get the message and go away. Other people, even ones who had the nerve to stand so close to the tigers, were free to look at them. They were huge creatures, magnificent and so graceful. As they lollygagged in the sun, it seemed incredible that they were capable of any ferocity. And yet of course they were, and Sage wasn't one to underestimate them. She had confronted enough creatures in the wild to have a tremendous respect for them.

"You'd probably feel right at home in there with them."

It was a disturbingly familiar voice, the kind that tickled the back of the neck with both excitement and warning. Sage whipped around, and for the first time in her life she gasped. He was there, Jackson Kirk, not just a figment of her imagination but very, very real. He had moved in close to her, trapping her between him and the tigers, but he didn't touch her. Dressed casually in jeans and a dark shirt with the sleeves rolled up to his elbows and with that tantalizing half smile on his face, he looked far more dangerous than the tigers. But were his intimidating looks just as misleading as their relaxed beauty?

"I just might be better off in with them," she said, finding herself maddeningly aware of his physical attraction. The sunlight made his eyes brighter, more disconcerting, more mysterious. "I'd hoped you'd given up on me."

"Not a chance."

"So my little inner voice kept telling me."

He studied her closely, as if the active mind behind those curious eyes was indeed contemplating pitching her to the tigers, an action that wouldn't have surprised Sage in the least. She looked away, however, unworried. Undoubtedly, if he put his mind to it, he could haul her up and toss her down among the wild beasts. He had the strength for the job, although she was by no means a weakling herself. But he wouldn't, not here. It was too crowded, too open. And she could be counted on to put up one heck of a fuss. Maybe they'd both end up down in the pit! Sage was so sure of herself that she resisted taking the involuntary step backward that would have been so natural in her situation.

Jackson Kirk acknowledged her stubborn bravery with a slight nod. "You're just as crazy as your grandfather. Maybe crazier."

"I wouldn't know. I hardly remember my grandfather."

"But I know him, and some things are obviously genetic."

"Obviously? But you don't know *me*, Kirk."

"I'm a quick judge of character."

She decided to change the subject, to try to do something about the probing way he was looking at her. She certainly didn't like what it was doing to her insides. She didn't need the added complication of the sexual energy that was flowing between them. It was distracting, dangerous, unwanted. "You followed me here from the hotel?"

"Mmm." The half smile softened, and there was a twinkle in his eyes. "It was remarkably simple. If you plan to keep this up, you'll have to improve your skills at skulduggery. I'm not an easy man to best, Sage. You might find it less taxing to cooperate."

"Give you the money, you mean."

He sighed. His faint smile began to disappear. "I made some mistakes last night, I admit. I'd like to make amends now if I can. Come on, let me buy you lunch. We'll talk."

"Seems I've heard that line before."

"This time I mean it."

Everything about him—his expression, his stance, his quiet, intense words—suggested he did, but Sage had no intention of being fooled. "I'll bet. What's the alternative?"

"To what?"

"To not going to lunch with you"

He laughed. "Eating alone."

She didn't believe him. If she refused, it just might be off to the tigers with her—and yet he suddenly looked so harmless, so intriguing and sincere. Maybe this time he did intend to talk. What harm could there be in giving him another chance? Besides, she was hungry.

She followed him down the wide sidewalk, crowded with happy zoogoers, and she wondered if other people had grandfathers who sent them weird telegrams asking for money. Mostly, though, she watched Jackson Kirk. He had an interesting way of walking—arresting, even. He didn't lumber, as so many big men did, or rush. Instead, he moved with grace and purpose and confidence, but not as if he owned the world or even cared to. More as if he didn't give a damn *who* owned the world. He was himself, and nothing was going to change that.

You're noticing far too much about Kirk, she warned herself. But then she rationalized that that wasn't necessarily true, since she needed to learn as much about the man as she could, through objective observation as well as listening and asking questions. What she needed to avoid was subjective observation—and reacting to what she observed. It just wouldn't do to hang back a little and think how incredibly sexy his walk was or relish the play of muscles in his long legs or the ratio of his broad shoulders to his lean hips or sigh at the way the sunlight danced on his dark hair. Those kinds of observations were decidedly subjective, not to mention dangerous.

They got cheeseburgers, fries and lemonade from a stand and sat at a table in the shade. Sage let him pay— she could afford her own lunch, but she didn't need to prove anything to him. Didn't want to. She duly noted that he carried a fine leather wallet, expensive, and she got a peek at a row of credit cards, an American Express Gold Card right on top. He obviously wasn't the sort who normally frequented seedy San Diego hotels. With his array of plastic he could have stayed anywhere in the city.

Of course, so could she. It was Grandpa Killibrew who had brought her—and Kirk, it seemed—to the Happy Trails Hotel.

"Did you know I'd be there last night, or were you just guessing?" she asked, squeezing ketchup onto her burger. Kirk looked on with distaste, eating his garnished only with lettuce and tomato.

"It was an educated guess. It stood to reason, your being Bradford Killibrew's granddaughter, that you'd show up a day early. He'd call it reconnoitering."

Sage frowned, thinking back to the strategy-planning session she'd held with herself shortly after receiving Grandpa's peculiar telegram. Reconnoiter was exactly the word she'd used. She was already suspicious of Kirk. Now she was getting irritated with him. He was entirely too smug for her tastes. Just a lucky guess, she told herself. "My grandfather didn't send you to pick up the money, did he? That was a lie."

Kirk laughed, and this time Sage had no chance to try to control her reaction. In an instant she took in everything—the luscious, deep sound, the flash of white teeth, the crinkling at the corners of his eyes. The impact on her senses was awesome. No man had a right to be that damned sexy. But Jackson Kirk was, and she would have to watch herself.

"No, I admit he didn't. Hardly." He laughed again, and Sage snatched up a french fry to distract herself. "Your grandfather likes playing games as much as you do."

"This is not a game, not as far as I'm concerned. I haven't enjoyed a single moment of any of it."

"Not even throwing that drink in my face?"

She thought back to last night, to the look of surprise on his face, and had to hold back a smile. It had been an impulsive but necessary act. "You didn't leave me much choice."

"And the towels? Tell me you didn't relish imagining my reaction when I opened your briefcase."

"Relish isn't the word, Kirk. I was—I *am* in an untenable situation. I don't know who you are. I don't know if you're dangerous. I don't even know if you really do know my grandfather. What I imagined when you opened the briefcase wasn't so much the look on your face as what you'd do next. I figured you'd burst into my room with a gun and demand the money—"

"Perhaps I should have. You have your grandfather's flair for the dramatic, I see."

She appraised him for a moment, as coolly and objectively as she could. "You don't believe me. You don't think I was afraid."

"No, I don't. Your 'little voice' would have told you not to be, not of me."

She supposed in a way it had, but she didn't appreciate Kirk's telling her so. He knew too much about her, guessed too much. It was disconcerting.

"You know, those towels only made me more determined," he told her quietly, his eyes impenetrable in the shadows. "If you'd just told me to go to hell, I might have let you and your grandfather sort this out on your own. But cheating me, being so sneaky and underhanded—" he paused, leaning back and smiling "—well, Sage Killibrew, that just brought out the fight in me."

She wasn't at all sure what to say.

He stretched out his long legs under the table, his toes just missing hers, and gave her a lingering look before picking up a french fry and slowly, deliberately biting it in two. "Now I wouldn't even dream of dropping this challenge."

"Fine," she said hotly, and even managed a regal shrug. "I don't give a damn what you do, Kirk. Just don't try to stop me from seeing my grandfather."

He made no reply, merely continuing to observe her with a lively but intensely controlled interest. Sage had the distinct feeling—no, she *knew*—that Jackson Kirk would do whatever he wanted to do. If he wanted to try to stop her, he would. If he wanted to leave her alone, he would. Clearly he was a man used to making his own decisions. In that regard they were alike.

"Are you going to tell me what kind of mess my grandfather's in?" she asked briskly.

"Not one even forty thousand dollars would resolve."

She'd been afraid of something like that and abruptly lost her appetite. For the first time she suspected Kirk was telling the truth. In the overall scheme of things, forty thousand dollars wasn't much.

"Where's the money, Sage?"

She scoffed. "Do you actually think I'd tell you?"

"If you had any sense—" He bit back his words, visibly reining in his impatience. "Look, I'm only trying to help."

"And I only have your word for that. Given the circumstances, I *would* be crazy if I decided to trust a perfect stranger—one who follows me around, no less—on the basis of only his word."

He wasn't listening. "It's not in your room."

Sage was momentarily taken aback. "What's not? How— The money, you mean?"

She stared at him as he began to smile, his eyebrows raised in sudden amusement, and she realized the implication of his words.

"I don't believe this!" She jumped to her feet. "You snuck into my room! You searched my belongings! You— How can you possibly expect me to trust you? What did you do, follow me here so you'd know where to find me, then double back to the hotel so you could search my room? How dare you!"

"Actually," he said with perfect calm, "I searched your room last night. You never even woke up."

She knocked the remainder of her lunch into his lap and stalked off, livid. Kirk made no move to follow her, but she wouldn't have cared if he had. She'd have turned him over to the first security guard she saw. Or pitched *him* to the tigers. She took very small comfort in knowing that he'd missed the money. Indeed, it wasn't just that he'd broken into her room that bothered her. It was that she distinctly recalled the air-conditioning had been inadequate.

So she'd slept in the nude. With the covers drawn back.

Reason, however, prevailed. Instead of storming out of the zoo and leaving herself open for another sneak attack from Jackson Kirk, halfway to the exit she shoved aside images of his cool gaze roving over her sleeping nude form and doubled back. Maybe last night he'd been so intent on the money that he hadn't noticed her!

He was finishing his lemonade in the shade. The picture of innocence, she thought with contempt. When he rose and threw away his trash, Sage hovered behind a tree, waiting. She didn't know what she'd accomplish, but it sure beat going back to the Happy Trails. Unless Kirk caught her. Then there'd be hell to pay, to be sure.

Finally he started toward the exit. There was nothing in his easy, nonchalant gait that revealed he'd just had half a cheeseburger and french fries dumped on him and hadn't yet gotten his way with Sage. So to speak, she thought with a sudden rush of heat.

Sage followed, keeping well behind him. He was taller than most of the zoo visitors and therefore easy to keep in sight. Outside the zoo he climbed into a black Alfa Romeo and drove off, leaving Sage standing alone in frustration. Big deal, she'd seen him leave the zoo! She wondered where he was going. To see Grandpa Killibrew? To plot against her? To try again for the money?

She needed a car, dammit.

But at least he was gone. She felt free. Safe. Back in control. No way was Jackson Kirk going to sneak up on her again!

Annoyed that her exploration of the zoo had been cut short, she took a cab to a car-rental agency, choosing an inconspicuous sedan. Then she headed downtown and bought another black briefcase, a cheap one on sale. Back at the hotel she removed the stacks of bills from the pillowcase, placed them in the briefcase and showered, with the briefcase within grabbing distance. She wasn't taking any chances.

For supper she ordered up some enchiladas and a bottle of Dos Equis beer. They arrived with a message from the front desk: Sage's best friend from Colorado, Diana, had called with an urgent request for Sage to call back at once.

Sage didn't bother to mention that she'd been in her room for nearly two hours. She figured she was lucky to get the message at all. Other than Jackson Kirk and presumably Grandpa Killibrew, Diana was the only person who knew where to find her. But Diana thought her hiking and skiing comrade was on a well-deserved vacation. Sage glanced around her tacky little room and took a sip of the mercifully cold beer. Some vacation.

Diana answered on the second ring. "Hi," Sage said, "it's me. What's up?"

"That's my line. You're moving out to San Diego, huh? That's what this trip's all about? Fink. I knew you left suddenly and all that and you were being awfully secretive, but you could have told me!"

"Diana! What are you talking about?" Sage set her beer on the nightstand. Now what? "I have no intention of moving."

"Hey, look, you don't have to lie, Sage. Bob called."

Neither Sage nor Diana had what could be called a steady job, although both made decent money and were well respected for their skills. Sometimes they worked for Bob at the ski lodge, giving lessons and patrolling the slopes. "And?"

"And he said some guy from San Diego had called checking into your salary and employment history, said you were applying for a job in San Diego and—"

"I'll be damned. *Kirk!*"

"Who?"

"Diana, did Bob tell this guy anything?"

"Well, yeah, sure. You okay?"

"*Damn* that man."

"Sage, you want to explain?"

"No. I mean—Lord. It's a long story, Diana, and I promise I'll tell you everything just as soon as I can. Remember my telling you about my eccentric grandfather? Well, this has to do with him and a certain male individual who . . . Oh, never mind."

"That would be Kirk," Diana said dryly, the anger and concern gone from her tone. She'd seen her friend demolish more than one interfering male.

"It would. Suffice it to say he wasn't on the level."

"Then you're not moving."

"No."

"You can if you want, you know, but we are friends and I just like to be told these things."

"Diana, Kirk just wanted to find out if I could come up with forty thousand in cash in a couple of days."

Diana started laughing so hard she couldn't say goodbye, so Sage just hung up. Forty thousand was a lot of money, but at least she could have come up with it if Grandpa had given her a little more time. But it would have entailed selling virtually everything she owned, except her land near Aspen, of course. Not for anyone would she sell her land. But forty thousand in three days? It had been a lot for dear old Grandpa Killibrew to expect, but she'd done her best.

She hoped it was good enough.

FOR HER FIRST MEETING with her grandfather in twenty years Sage dressed in a blue jumpsuit with a wide belt, sandstone earrings and sandals. She felt all grown up, and yet like a little girl.

She could remember so vividly the last time she'd seen this man who'd left his thumbprint so firmly, so permanently, on them all: her father, who was off roaming the South Pacific with his doctor-wife, supplying care and medicine to the needy; her uncle Summerfield, who had thrown his all into reviving Summerfield Shoe, the company that had provided the underpinning of the family fortune that Grandpa had abandoned years ago; her sister, Juniper, who worked long, hard hours at Killibrew Traders, the company Grandpa had founded and built up after bailing out of shoes. And even old Auntie Killibrew, Grandpa's sister, the starch and rock of the family. They all had memories of Bradford Killibrew. They all had been affected by his departure. In all of them, Sage included, there was the urge to do something out of the ordinary, to strike out into new territory, to take risks. It was in the Killibrew blood. And it was virtually all Grandpa had given them.

Somehow they'd been able to understand his departure, even without knowing the particulars of why he'd left or where he'd gone.

He'd seemed brash and victorious that last day, full of life but already old to a child of seven. He'd held Sage on his lap—Juniper was too big, she remembered—and let her pull the hairs poking out his open-necked shirt. He'd chuckled and kissed her on the cheek when he told her goodbye. She'd thought he meant for the night, not forever.

"For twenty years," she said aloud, surprised at the note of wistfulness in her voice.

No one had ever been able to explain adequately to her what had happened to him. It wasn't until she was older that Sage realized the adults around her hadn't been able to throw any light on his disappearance because they themselves had no explanations. No one knew where Grandpa Killibrew was.

Even now no one knew. Certainly Sage didn't.

But when she'd felt the stirrings in her own soul to seek adventure, to do the unusual, and saw that quality in those she loved, she'd understood her long lost grandfather. He hadn't left to hurt them. He'd left because he had to, for whatever reasons.

Shoving memories aside, Sage grabbed her briefcase and went down to the lobby. It was five minutes before nine. She stood outside the swinging doors to the bar, took a deep breath and pushed them open.

It was dark and quiet, populated by an unsavory group similar to the one there the previous night. Kirk's "men" were even there—fakes, of course. They no more worked for him than they did for her. He'd just tried to shake her confidence, bend her to his will. Fat lot of good it'd done him!

Sage sat at the same table as the night before, ordering another Dos Equis as she tucked the briefcase between her feet. She looked around for Jackson Kirk, and she looked around for an old man who might be Bradford Killibrew.

And, not seeing either of them, she waited.

At nine-thirty she'd finished her beer and ordered coffee. She just kept it in front of her, not touching it. She would wait another thirty minutes. Then she would check out of this damned fleabag of a hotel, drive to the airport, get rid of her rented car and buy a ticket for the first plane to Colorado. By then she would have had enough of this nonsense. She'd had damned near enough of it right now.

The doors to the lobby swung open, and Sage held her breath. Given her string of bad luck, it would be Kirk.

He'd take the briefcase, inspect the contents right there in the bar with her looking on and have it out with her once and for all. And he wouldn't be pleased. No, he certainly wouldn't. Men like that didn't like to be led on wild-goose chases.

But it wasn't Kirk who came through those swinging doors and strode into the lounge. This man was tall, very lean, wiry and white-haired. He wore patched khakis that hung on his lanky frame and a brightly patterned Hawaiian shirt. As he moved into the lounge, a ray of light from the bar area struck his face, and Sage saw the familiar deep blue eyes, the same color as hers.

Bradford Killibrew ordered a beer.

Grandpa.

3

BRADFORD KILLIBREW RECOGNIZED his granddaughter at
once, and a broad grin broke across his face. With carefree grace he walked over to her table and sat down, and
he chuckled a little and shook his head as he spoke.
"Well, Sage," he said, raising his beer glass. "Cheers."

"Cheers," she said hoarsely and raised her cup.

Nothing about Bradford Killibrew suggested the ur-
gency of his telegram, or even his past as one of the most
prominent business executives in New England. His skin
was bronzed, setting off his white hair and bushy white
eyebrows, the muscles in his lean arms were sinewy and
he had big powerful hands with surprisingly long fingers, at first glance almost delicate-looking. He had on
Killibrew Traders deck shoes. Sage wanted to laugh
aloud, but nothing came out. Juniper would go crazy
when she found out! After all Grandpa Killibrew had
done—his abrupt departure from the family company
and the family itself, his long, long silence and now his
sudden reappearance—he could still tramp around in the
shoes he'd once sold for a living. Although Sage couldn't
blame him for wanting to get out of that particular
racket—she'd vowed never to work a single minute at
Killibrew Traders and thus far hadn't.

And contrary to the rumors that had circulated about
him over the years, Grandpa looked neither infirm nor
insane. In fact, he looked damned content with his lot.
Maybe he really had spent time with cannibals in South

America, desperadoes and gold prospectors in Mexico, Hindu monks in Asia—all of which, at one time or another, he'd supposedly been spotted doing.

Sage didn't know what to say. She only knew that no matter how she and the rest of the family might feel about his absence, no matter what his reasons were for it, she couldn't be angry with him. He looked too fit, too content, too perfectly at home with himself and the world. She could only hope for as much for herself when she reached his age. And he was her grandfather. That said it all.

"Grandpa," she said and drank.

He laughed, bringing back memories of her childhood, picnics and trips to his office—and of her grandmother, whom he'd loved to tease. They'd laughed so much together over the years. Everyone said so, and Sage herself remembered it. She could still see her, clearly and vividly.

"See why I cabled you and no one else?" His voice was gruff and sandpapery. The smooth veneer of the Yankee businessman was gone. "Juniper would have hog-tied me until I answered every last question she had listed in that all-business head of hers, your father never has any money and Summerfield would have thought the whole thing a big joke and laughed his butt off while he tore up my telegram."

Sage smiled—how well he knew them! "What about Auntie?"

"She'd have shot me dead."

It was probably only a slight exaggeration. At the very least, Sage's great-aunt, a retired schoolteacher, would have broken her brother's beer glass over his head, humphed and stalked out. Auntie wasn't one for wasting words when actions would suffice.

"So." Grandpa gulped some beer and looked at her with his beady blue eyes. "You brought the money?"

Sage licked her lips, suddenly gone dry. "Four hundred one-hundred dollar bills."

"Cash on the barrel! Yep, Sage, I knew I could count on you. Let's have the briefcase. I'll get this thing settled, and you and me will head out to Disneyland for a day and I'll explain the whole rotten mess."

Disneyland. She sighed, shaking her head. Did he still think she was seven?

"Always wanted to take you to Disneyland," he said, reading her thoughts. "Better late than never, I figure."

"Grandpa—Grandpa, it's not going to be that simple."

His eyes flashed at her. "Beg pardon?"

"The forty thousand. It's mostly Monopoly money. Monopoly, Jeopardy, Careers—I raided the games at the lodge. Most of it's hundreds, though. I couldn't—"

"Monopoly money?" he repeated, dumbfounded. "Why?"

"Bulk, size, my sense of the dramatic. I wanted my stacks to be convincing, in case worse came to worst, which it may have. I've got real hundreds on the top— eight of them—for appearances. I had no idea what I'd run into. As it is, I nearly had *them* stolen. You can imagine if I'd been carting around forty thousand."

"Eight hundred dollars. That's all you brought?"

He seemed more incredulous than disappointed, and certainly not angry. Sage nodded. "That's all I have in cash. I also have a bank check for ten thousand. It's in my handbag. Grandpa, it would have been insane to bring that much cash. But I can get cash if you need it."

"Ten thousand isn't near enough. Neither's forty, probably, but I had to try."

"I don't have forty thousand in cash and couldn't get it by tonight."

He looked at her. "You did a couple of weeks ago. I checked. What happened?"

Bile and beer rose in her throat. "Then that's why you contacted me—because I had the cash! Well, for your information, Grandfather, I just used it as a down payment on a piece of land. I was damned lucky to come up with the ten. Since it means so little to you—"

"Now hold on, hold on." He reached across the table and grabbed her wrist, pulling her down as she started to get up. "Juniper could have come up with the money, too. Checked her out *and* Sum *and* your dad. So don't get all huffy. Didn't want to ask you to do something you couldn't have done—which I ended up doing, anyway." He let go of her hand and drank some more beer, contemplating. "Well, damn."

"I can call Juniper," Sage offered.

"Too late for that."

"Are you going to tell me what's going on?"

"Let me think a minute."

Sage considered bringing up the name Jackson Kirk, but she didn't and drank some of her coffee instead, keeping silent. Let him think. Let him decide on his own to tell her everything: why he needed the money, why Jackson Kirk wanted it, who Kirk was. He had to. She'd gone out of her way to help him. He *owed* her an explanation.

Of course, obligation and responsibility had never meant much to Bradford Killibrew. He danced to his own tune.

"Grandpa," she asked quietly, "did you honestly expect me to bring cash?"

He looked at her and smiled, shaking his head. "Honestly? No, I can't say I did."

"But you did expect forty grand."

"Wanted it, Sage," he said, a distant look coming into his eyes. "Desperately."

"I'm sorry. I, well, to be honest, Grandpa, I thought this was just a joke. I didn't really take our telegram seriously. I thought it was just some scheme you'd cooked up to make your homecoming more dramatic, not that you needed one. Until Jackson Kirk showed up—"

"*Kirk!*"

Sage winced as her grandfather's face reddened. "Oh, dear. I take it he's not a friend of yours."

"A friend!" he boomed. "Why, that rascal—"

But suddenly the rascal was there. Neither Sage nor her grandfather had noticed his entrance. It was as if he'd materialized from thin air, dark, unsmiling, violet eyes riveted on Sage, not on Bradford Killibrew.

She didn't know what to say, and before she could think of anything, Kirk grabbed her shoulders. Turning redder and redder, Grandpa stared furiously from across the table.

"Listen here, Kirk," he ordered.

Jackson ignored Grandpa, warmth coming into his eyes as a tantalizing half smile softened his hard features, and she became absorbed in his sheer presence. "Sage," he said, his voice curiously seductive.

She pushed back her chair, but his hands remained on her shoulders, his grip secure, but not harsh. She supposed she could get away if she thought there was anything threatening about his hold or his intentions. If, she admitted, she wanted to. But his eyes held her as surely as his hands, and she gazed at him, mesmerized, her heart beating with vague anticipation. She was hardly aware of her grandfather.

Her inner voice demanded to know what the devil was going on, if she was crazy, nuts, gone out of her head. Only seconds had passed since Kirk had grabbed her, but they were slow seconds, to be imprinted, she knew, in her mind forever.

You should listen to your little voice, she tried to tell herself.

But it was too late. Jackson lowered his mouth to hers, which was still wide open in shock. Across the table Grandpa grunted ominously, but there was nothing either of them could do. Sage wanted the touch of Jackson Kirk's lips on hers, she realized, somewhat dazed. His tongue flicked against hers. The kiss was hot and liquid and spine-tingling.... *And under very different circumstances you might just lean back and enjoy it, but not now!*

Her inner voice again. This time Sage listened. She backed up sharply, the chair slamming against the wall, but Jackson followed, his mouth never leaving hers.

Grandpa smacked his hand on the tabletop and jumped to his feet, cursing wildly. "So you've already gotten to her, have you, Kirk?" he yelled. "My own granddaughter!"

She snatched her mouth away. "No—"

"Well," Grandpa sputtered. "Dammit, man, don't think you've heard the last of me!"

"*Grandpa!*"

She started up but ran into the solid wall of Jackson's six-foot-plus frame. He was bending down, sliding one hand down between her knees, for no other purpose than to grab her briefcase. She slammed her legs together, trying to hold the briefcase with her ankles, but he plucked it away.

In the thrill of his victory he dropped his other hand from her shoulder, and Sage immediately ducked between him and the empty chair behind her, kicking it out of her way and leaping out of the long reach of his arm. He could have the damned briefcase! She dashed after her grandfather.

He was already out on the street, moving fast. Sage grabbed him by the arm. "That wasn't me," she said quickly. "That was him, his idea, believe me. He's after the money. He told me he was a friend of yours and tried for it last night, but I—"

The old man snorted in disbelief and anger. "The conniving cad!"

"Please believe me."

"Of course I do." His voice softened, but he spoke rapidly, "Dammit, I've obviously miscalculated. Get yourself out of this hotel, Sage. It's safe enough, if a bit ragged, but now that Kirk knows you're here . . . Go to the Hotel del Coronado, check in. I'll get in touch with you there."

"Okay, but what about Kirk? He'll be out here any second."

The hotel door swung open and Kirk ran out. *"Killibrew!"*

"Don't let him follow me," Grandpa whispered. "You can handle him."

"What! Grandpa—"

"He's not dangerous to people," he added mysteriously and pelted down the street with an agility that belied his years.

Jackson Kirk was fuming. Briefcase firmly in hand, he dove after the old man and completely ignored Sage—

his mistake. She stuck out a foot and tripped him. He went flying, and the briefcase crashed to the sidewalk and burst open.

Fake money flew everywhere. Purple, green, tan, gold. Sage wanted to laugh. What had she gotten herself into? But she didn't waste time. While Kirk painfully picked himself up off the sidewalk, cursing madly, she snatched up the real one-hundred dollar bills and tucked them into a pocket.

Jackson ended his string of oaths with an utterly final, vehement "Damn!" He glared with ferocity at the empty street where Bradford Killibrew had disappeared into the night. Then he glared at her, swooped down and scooped up a handful of the fake money. He threw it as far as he could.

Sage couldn't hold back a chuckle as the money wafted back down to the sidewalk in the cool night air.

"Lady," Jackson snapped, breathing hard, and grabbed her by the elbow, "it's high time we had us a little chat."

Feeling victorious but breathing hard herself, Sage wrested herself from his grip. "I've heard that line from you before, Kirk, and as I recall, it got me nowhere. I'm on my grandfather's side. Whatever trouble he's in, whatever you have against him, he's my grandfather."

"Dammit, I'm on his side, too!"

"He begs to differ."

"He's a crazy old man!" Jackson was clearly enraged. "And you—you're nuts, as well. How I ever became involved with you two . . ."

Sage gave him a cold look, despite the churning in her stomach. One dark lock hung wildly down his forehead and his violet eyes gleamed with intensity, but she could feel the tangle of emotions at work in him. And still the unresolved sexual tension was almost palpable. She felt as if she might catch fire at any moment, and if he touched her again.... She backed up a step, to see to it that he wouldn't.

"You tried to steal forty thousand dollars, Kirk," she said, avoiding the eyes that seemed to penetrate her facade. Did he know she thought he was incredibly sexy? "I should call the police."

He laughed thinly, his gaze roving over her briefly, then he indicated the scattered money with one contemptuous nod. "And show them your booty—a briefcase full of Monopoly money? Then who'd have the last laugh?" He tossed back his head, groaning up at the night sky. "Oh, hell." He looked at her again, serious now, back in control of himself. "Look, Sage, I was just trying to stop your grandfather from doing something he and I both know won't work—and could only aggravate his situation. I am not his enemy."

His words were utterly final, all the more convincing because they were so evenly delivered, his eyes never leaving hers. Sage was keenly aware that she wanted to believe him, and that in and of itself was dangerous. "Take that up with him."

He studied her for a moment, then reached out and brushed the top of her hand with two fingers. Sensations radiated outward from his touch, shooting through her body, but she forced herself not to move, not to show him what he did to her. "I'll tell you everything over a drink," he said seductively. "Promise."

Obviously he already had his own ideas about what he did to her. "No third chances," she said firmly. "Grandpa says you're not dangerous—and maybe you're not. But you're obviously a liar. Just give up, Kirk."

She could see his self-control rapidly diminishing, giving her some measure of hope.

"Dammit, why even bother talking?" he muttered. "You'd probably think his scheme made sense."

But Sage refused to be tempted. She knew better than to think he was going to tell her anything. She would check into the Hotel del Coronado and wait for her grandfather's call. It was the only solution.

"I'm not listening," she said.

Jackson exploded, throwing his hands up in disgust. "You're both crazy and bullheaded. Go ahead—side with your grandfather, don't listen to reason, don't give a sane man the chance to apologize and start fresh." His face darkened. "Dammit, go on and go up to your room and leave me with a sidewalk full of play money!"

"You didn't think I'd come to a place like this with real money, did you?" She was goading him, and he knew it.

"Don't push me too far, Sage," he said, his voice suddenly dead quiet. "You could regret it."

"You're right." She tried to keep her tone light, a little smug. To pull it off, she had to look away from him. "I think I will go on up to my room." And she headed inside.

She was halfway to the entrance when he called softly, "By the way." Something in his voice compelled her to turn, and when she did, she saw he was curiously calm. He grinned—slyly, sensuously, just enough to make her blood burn with a longing she didn't want to feel. He went on, deliberate, sensual. "No apology for the kiss. I'd do it again."

Her knees went weak, but she replied stonily, "I'm sure you would."

"I plan to."

She had no choice but to leave him with the last word—and a sidewalk full of play money, her only consolation. Annoyed with him *and* herself, she slammed the door on her way into the hotel. The strength in her weakened knees didn't return until some time after she arrived in her room. At least, she thought, he didn't get her eight hundred dollars—or her grandfather.

THE HOTEL DEL CORONADO, popularly known as the Hotel Del, is located across San Diego Bay on the lovely Coronado Peninsula. As far as Sage was concerned, it was about a million steps up from the Happy Trails. The Del opened its doors a century ago and immediately became one of the greatest Pacific Coast resort hotels, and Sage welcomed its touch of history and continuity in such a "new" city. The Spanish influence in the hotel's design and overall ambience of plushness and luxury had a relaxing effect on her, prompting her to splurge on an oceanfront room.

As she showered and tried to calm down, Sage considered all the aggravation Grandpa Killibrew and Jackson Kirk had caused her and wondered why she didn't just pack and go home. Was it simple curiosity that was luring her into staying? Some weird sense of family duty? Adventure? Risk? Insanity?

Probably the Killibrew genes, she thought, and snuggled down under the covers. She tried to dismiss Jackson Kirk as The Enemy. Tried not to think about his alluring violet eyes and sexy scar and tall, hard frame. He was Grandpa's nemesis, and therefore her own.

Nothing, however, could be that simple. Warm and relaxed, Sage had to admit she honestly didn't know either man. Both could be lying...or neither. Both could be using her...or neither. Grandpa was everything and nothing she'd expected. He seemed mentally competent and he definitely intrigued her, but so far his presence had added to the questions she'd had for twenty years, not subtracted. Where had he been the past two decades? What had he been doing? And what kind of trouble was he in that forty thousand dollars only *might* help?

Blood tied her to her grandfather. Yet something just as elemental—maybe more so—drew her inexorably to Jackson Kirk: a deep, basic, undeniable physical attraction. It presented itself, dangerous and irresistible, whenever she was near him, whenever she thought about him. But neither blood nor sex was a rational basis on which to decide whom to trust, whom to listen to, whom to help.

Therefore, she had to act.

She could no longer afford to let Grandpa or Kirk try to manipulate her into doing their will. She had to take control. If her conscience wouldn't let her return to Colorado and forget what was going on here, then she had to take matters into her own hands and find out for herself without waiting for either man to get around to telling her what she wanted to know. She'd play detective. Ask questions, demand answers, look for clues, compile the facts into a clear picture.

And, by God, she'd get started right now!

She switched on a light and began flipping through the phone book. No Bradford Killibrew was listed anywhere in or near San Diego—hardly a surprise but worth checking.

A Jackson Kirk, however, was.

Right there on Coronado.

"Ha!" she said aloud, victorious. She memorized the address with a certain glee, then finally snuggled back down under the covers...and again felt the hands of her violet-eyed stranger on her shoulders, the pressure and liquid warmth of his mouth on hers. She was feeling so smug after discovering his address that she just gave herself up to the sensations of her vivid memory and soon, sighing peacefully, drifted off to sleep.

Yes, she thought dreamily, attraction could present its own difficulties, but she was confident that in the end she wouldn't give in to her impulsive nature—to the Killibrew in her, as Juniper would say. Her common sense would prevail.

She'd pay Kirk a visit in the morning. Bright and early.

4

GRANDPA KILLIBREW SHATTERED all Sage's plans by phoning her at seven in the morning and commanding her to meet him on the terrace in thirty minutes for breakfast. "You could ask nicely," she told him, miffed. "I don't like being ordered about."

He laughed. "Of course you don't. You're a Killibrew."

"Then—"

"Be there." He hung up.

Sage was running out of clothes. She hadn't brought many with her, and in any case, her wardrobe wasn't equipped to handle the life-style of a resort hotel in a warm climate, but she thought her crisp white skirt and white canvas shirt were more than presentable. She wondered if she could take time out from her skulduggery to do laundry. Did Sam Spade ever worry about such mundane details?

With her hair still damp from her quick shower, she breezed down to the terrace. It was the kind of warm, gorgeous day that made her wonder why she lived in Colorado. There was no chill in the breeze from the ocean, and she loved its smell—tangy, misty, invigorating.

Bradford Killibrew was sitting in a quiet corner by himself. He looked clean and pressed and quite dapper. Sage surprised him by telling him so.

"You're no sorry sight yourself," he said, smiling that smile that could make virtually anyone forgive him his faults. "Sit down. What'll it be for breakfast?"

"Just fresh fruit, a muffin and hot tea."

"You can afford this place?"

"You should know, you checked out my finances."

Hurt clouded his vivid eyes. "Sage—"

"I'm sorry, Grandpa. I managed to get my eight hundred back from Kirk."

"Ah, Kirk. The wretch."

Wretch? Sage unfolded her napkin on her lap and forced herself to keep quiet until they had ordered their breakfasts, which were obviously going to be on her. It was the first indication of Grandpa's former habits—he'd always been known to be a penny-pincher. Either that, she thought, or he was truly impoverished.

"Sage." He sighed, making a pyramid with his bronzed elbows and folded hands. "I've been thinking. Maybe— No, not maybe. Sage you should just forget about me and go home. I've no business involving you in my troubles after all these years."

Their breakfasts arrived—Grandpa had ordered a monstrous one—and Sage fixed her tea, glad she hadn't told him about last night's resolution. "I already am involved."

He peppered everything on his plate. "But you don't know anything."

"Jackson Kirk doesn't believe that."

"Doesn't matter what that shyster believes. I'll keep him occupied while you make your exit."

The muffin was fresh and absolutely fabulous, and with the fresh air and her long lost grandfather sitting across from her, Sage couldn't find it in herself to get upset. In his position, after last night she'd have wanted her out of there, too. But she wasn't leaving.

"Who is he?" she asked.

Grandpa grunted. "So he hasn't even told you that much, has he?"

"Like you, Grandpa, he hasn't told me a blessed thing."

"Then that business last night . . ." He bit into a peppered slice of whole wheat toast. "You two aren't—"

"Of course not."

He peered at her as he chewed thoughtfully. "I didn't think so. I suppose I wondered at first, Jackson Kirk being what he is and you being what you are, but—"

"What do you mean, me being what I am?"

"You know, impulsive. Damn the torpedoes and full speed ahead."

"Grandpa, I'm not the bratty little girl you knew twenty years ago."

"Maybe not, but who responded to her grandpa's crazy telegram? Who came traipsing out here with a briefcase full of play money?"

"You asked me to come."

"And so you did. Exactly my point."

"Well, it doesn't matter." She drank some tea and just wanted to lean back and close her eyes and breathe in the ocean air. But she kept her gaze fixed on the old man across from her. "Kirk was just trying to manipulate me—and you."

That got another grunt. "He's a fiend, that one."

A fiend and a wretch. *She* could think up her own names for Jackson Kirk. So far she wasn't getting anywhere. "What does he want with you?"

"The more I tell you, the more you'll want to stay."

"I've already made up my mind to stay, Grandpa. Telling me what's going on isn't going to change that—I'll figure it out myself if I have to."

His beady eyes narrowed, piercing her with the intelligence and insight she remembered from her childhood. This was the astute businessman who had launched a nationally known catalog company and used to dress in gray suits virtually seven days a week. Sage warned herself she shouldn't underestimate him.

"You mean it, don't you?" he asked.

She nodded. "I do."

"All right." He told her bluntly, "Your Jackson Kirk wants to stop me from getting my paintings back."

"Your what?"

"My paintings."

"You're an art dealer? A collector?"

"No, I'm a painter." He said it matter-of-factly, without pride or affectation; that was what he was. "That's what I've been doing all these years—painting."

When she thought of him in his massive Portsmouth office, his shirtsleeves rolled up to his elbows, she couldn't see it. No, it was impossible. He'd been a hard-nosed Yankee businessman. An eccentric, perhaps, wild and brash and all that, but definitely not a painter. An artist, for heaven's sake. Of all the rumors of what he'd become, that particular occupation hadn't even hit the list.

Yet when she looked at him now, casual and lean and at peace with himself, at least, if not the world, she could see him with paintbrush in hand, easel in front of him, palette spread with color. She couldn't imagine his work, but she could imagine him *at* work. It was a beginning.

"These paintings you want back . . . Kirk has them?"

"Not exactly, no."

"Then who does?"

"Someone he knows. A cohort of his, you might say."

"I see." She didn't but realized information was going to be hard to come by. Grandpa obviously didn't relish discussing this particular topic. He was stiffening up and ignoring what was left of his breakfast. Sage asked, "The forty thousand would have bought them back?"

"By my accounts, yes, but, well, the best laid plans of mice and men, you know." He stood absently, came around the table and kissed her on the forehead. "Now I'm going to have to put Plan B into operation, and you'll be relieved to know that it doesn't call for your help. You've been a charm, Sage m'dear, but I knew you would be. Love to the family. I'll turn up one of these days and shock the hell out of 'em. Meanwhile, you never mind me or this Jackson Kirk devil. Take care of yourself and get the blazes out of here."

"Grandpa, I just told you—"

"And I just told *you*."

"Give me a hint. This Plan B doesn't require forty grand?"

He grinned then, the breeze lifting his snow-white hair, and he smiled, a rich, cocky smile that filled his face with energy and mischief. He was a determined old man, but then, Sage recalled, he always had been. "Doesn't require a cent."

"Grandpa—"

The smile vanished so suddenly it might never have been there, and tears came into his bright eyes, as if he couldn't believe he was a grandfather, had been gone that long, had been gone at all. "I love the sound of that. Say it once more, Sage."

Her heart swelled with love for him. "Grandpa."

"Good. As for the paintings, if I can't buy them back—" his cocky grin returned "—then I'll just have to steal them, won't I?"

He strutted off, leaving her there with her tea and half-eaten muffin. "Damn you, old man," she muttered and leaped up. She followed him out to his car, badgering, cajoling, pleading—and having no effect whatsoever on his stubborn silence. "Colorado's a grand state" was the most she could get out of him. Thanking her for breakfast, he climbed into a big boat of a car that was mostly a pile of rust.

"I'd forgotten what tenacious, meddlesome lot the Killibrews are," he said good-naturedly through his open window, which he probably couldn't have shut if he'd wanted to. He used to drive late-model Cadillacs, Sage remembered. He chuckled at her. "No wonder I left."

And he was off. Sage got his license number and returned to her breakfast. Her tea was cold. She ordered a fresh pot and another muffin and sat thinking. If Grandpa could have a Plan B, then so could she.

AFTER BREAKFAST SAGE GOT a map from the hotel and studied it in her room. Coronado was a small enough island that finding the street listed beside Jackson Kirk's name in the telephone book was no problem. It was near the water, and she drove her nondescript rental car out there, finding it without making a single wrong turn. The white stucco house wasn't ostentatious, but it was no cottage, either. The small yard was beautifully landscaped with perennials and shrubs, and as Sage ambled up the walk, she noticed the place had a feeling of calm and relaxation and welcome—unlike Jackson Kirk himself. Perhaps she had the wrong Jackson Kirk?

But she noticed the black Alfa Romeo in the driveway and remembered it zooming away from her yesterday afternoon. Seeing it brought vividly to mind the man she was about to confront.

Maybe Grandpa was right. Maybe she should leave San Diego.

She had a choice between a doorbell and a knocker, and chose the doorbell. Waiting wasn't one of her preferred pastimes. She fiddled with her hair, counted to thirty and tried the knocker. Perhaps the doorbell didn't work.

"I'm on the terrace out back."

His voice behind her startled her, and when she whirled around, there he was. Her heart pounded uncontrollably, harder than it ever had before. She'd been caught in blizzards in the mountains, rescued stranded skiers, gone hang gliding and white-water rafting, but those were adventures, feats well within her capabilities. Coping with Jackson Kirk was another matter altogether.

And clad in gray sweatpants and a white tank top that emphasized every inch of his hard body, he gave a reason for her heart to pound. While consciously forcing herself to shut her mouth and be sensible, Sage noted the well-defined muscles in his tanned arms, the smoothness and strength of his shoulders, the flatness of his stomach under the lightweight shirt, slightly damp with perspiration. His legs seemed endless and he had on white running shoes. His eyes were clear and stunning, and all she could think about was how much she wanted to feel the warmth of his mouth on hers.

Watch yourself, Killibrew. She took a breath, vowing she would. "Morning," she said politely.

"Morning." His eyes glistened in the morning sun, telling her as if with words that he knew what she'd been thinking. "I heard you drive up. Got back a few minutes ago from jogging on the beach."

"Far?"

He laughed softly, without conceit. "You wouldn't stand so close if I'd gone far. No, I just wanted to loosen up. And think."

If Grandpa hadn't gotten her up for breakfast, Sage might have started her day with a run on the beach. She was athletic, used to being outdoors. She'd been over-indulging the past few days, and a good run might have cleared more out of her mind and body than just the effects of spicy foods, alcohol and inactivity.

"I suppose you have your own boat, too?"

"Mmm."

"The southern California life."

"Your grandfather's an expert yachtsman."

She smiled. "An echo of his former self. When he was in Portsmouth, he used to love to take us out—Juniper and me, that is. Juniper's my older sister. Our parents live on a boat. I guess it's in the blood."

"But you live in the mountains."

"I'm young yet. There's plenty of time for new adventures."

Something changed in his expression, nothing so simple as a softening or hardening of features, but something new, something that seemed to offer a glimpse at what made Jackson Kirk tick. Sage found herself fascinated by the change, wanting to know more. And then it was gone. He was hard-eyed and unreadable once more.

"Let's go out back," he said.

Since she wanted to talk to him, she decided to be agreeable and followed him without argument. He pointed to a plastic-coated metal deck chair, one of several scattered on the brick terrace. When she sat down, she felt as if she was enveloped by the lush greenery and flowering plants. She breathed in their scent, enjoying the way the sweetness mixed with the tang of the nearby ocean. Jackson grabbed a white towel from his chair and wiped the sweat off his face. She wished he hadn't. He looked even sexier with it, more human, more vulnerable.

"I'd decided to wash my hands of you, you know," he said, sitting down.

She shrugged. "A wise and rational decision, I'm sure."

His eyes, filled with warmth and color and mystery, fastened on her. "But one I could never stick to."

"Probably not."

He rocked back in his chair. "That sure of yourself, are you?"

She didn't like the undertone of amusement in his deep voice but suddenly realized he'd given their dialogue a romantic flavor—or, more precisely, a sexual one. Romance, that meeting of souls, hadn't entered their relationship. It rarely did, she reminded herself, with rogues like him. But he'd felt the tension, too. She wasn't heartened.

"I'm sure of you," she replied evenly. "You won't stop trying to prevent my grandfather from recovering his paintings, and you won't risk that I might know more than I've let on. You're as tenacious as I am, Jackson Kirk. You've proved that on several occasions already."

He refused to let her goad him. "So you know about the paintings, do you? Well, it doesn't matter what you know or don't know, Sage. The money in that briefcase wasn't real. You're no help—or threat—to your grand-father."

"Or to you?"

"Or to me."

She kicked out her legs and stretched. "Maybe I'd al-ready given my grandfather the real money and the play money was just to distract you. Do I look like the type to carry around forty thousand in cash in a place like the Happy Trails Hotel? In any place, for that matter?"

He leaned forward, casual and unworried, and slowly took in every inch of her frame, and she cursed herself for phrasing her question as she had. Then he smiled, not a big smile, but not that half smile, either; this one was filled with challenge and amusement. "Yes," he said, "you damn well do look the type."

Instead of letting him see he'd gotten to her, she tossed her head and kept her mind on business. "Well, that's neither here nor there," she said crisply. *Treat him like one of your teenagers*, she told herself. *Keep it simple and don't be lured off the subject.* "What I'm interested in, Mr. Kirk, is precisely how you learned I was meeting my grandfather, how you learned where I was meeting him and when and how you learned I'd be bringing money in a black briefcase."

"Ahh, then he hasn't told you."

She considered lying, pretending she knew more than she did to try to manipulate him into filling in the blanks, but she'd never been very good at lying. And she didn't think it would work, not with Jackson Kirk. *He* was good at lying. With a direct, uncompromising look she said, "No, he hasn't."

"I see." In a languid motion he brought one foot up and set it on his other knee. "Then you know little or noth-ing about the paintings."

Instantly she saw she'd miscalculated—she should have lied. "I know enough."

He laughed, rose, walked over to her and tapped her on the chin. She swallowed hard, resisting the impulses that already reigned over her senses and threatened to take over her mind, as well. His finger remained on her chin. "You don't know anything," he said. "And what your grandfather hasn't seen fit to tell you, neither do I. You're fishing, Sage Killibrew, and I'm not biting."

He strutted off, towel around his neck, cocky as hell. Sage leaped to her feet. "Wait!"

"I'm going to shower and change," he said, still walking as he turned to her. "When I'm done, I want you out. Did old Grandpa Killibrew send you packing when he found out you couldn't come up with the cash?" He nodded knowingly when he read her expression, which she thought she'd made *un*readable. "It figures. He's a solitary old cuss. See you, Sage."

She stood her ground. "I'm not leaving until we've had a chance to talk."

"Talk?" His voice deepened, and he went on seductively, "Darlin', if I come out of my shower and you're still here, the very last thing we'll do is talk."

"Don't threaten me!"

He stopped in the middle of the walk. "You know as well as I do what is a threat and what isn't."

She fought the urge to run—to him or away from him, she wasn't sure which. "I won't give you the satisfaction of asking you to clarify. I'll just tell you this: I'm here to help my grandfather. *That is all.*"

"Right. Say it a few more times, and maybe you'll convince yourself—but you won't convince me. That kiss last night convinced me of everything I need to know." He wiped his neck with a corner of the towel. "Be gone by the time I'm out of the shower."

He turned and sauntered inside, leaving Sage standing on the terrace, muttering at his straight back and nice firm behind. The man, she thought, was a menace.

5

SAGE HAD NEVER BEEN GOOD at taking orders. As soon as she figured Jackson was safely in the shower, she snuck in through the back door. She wasn't nervous. A man like Kirk would take long showers. Tiptoeing through the kitchen, which was big and sunny with oak cabinets and marble countertops and a breakfast nook overlooking the terrace, she went into a dining room that melted into a living room. Both were simply furnished, as clean and spare as the man who owned them, with fresh white walls and hardwood floors. There were two white love seats in the living room, and the few side pieces were beautifully crafted, expensive and unique. A hand-crafted Nepalese rug, exquisite in its detail, hung on one otherwise stark wall. There was no theme to the decor; Jackson Kirk obviously chose what he liked and damned the rules.

From the living room she crossed a ceramic tiled foyer, where a straight painted staircase led to the second floor. In the silent house she could hear the sounds of the shower and stood still for a moment, imagining him soaping up his tanned body…imagining herself in there with him.

Her inner voice told her such imaginings were not only treacherous, but also futile. They wouldn't get her anywhere.

She headed across the foyer into a smaller, somewhat darker room—the library. There was a big stone fireplace on the short back wall. Built-in shelves around it were filled with a variety of books. The furnishings were wood and leather and old, radiating a strong Spanish influence, and the atmosphere was cozier than that of the other rooms. It looked and felt like a room that was used often, and well.

Above a leather sofa was a painting that struck Sage with its daring yet careful use of color and line—a seascape. She'd never seen one quite like it, although she was no expert in art. On the surface the sea seemed quiet and isolated, friendly, and yet she could sense, too, its unpredictability. It seemed ready to burst forth at any moment with all its ferocity and power, to bring not peace, but death and destruction. It wasn't an easy painting. It wasn't soothing.

The scrawl in the lower right corner might have been Killibrew. Then again, it might not.

She went back into the foyer and down a short hall in the center of the house, returning to the kitchen. An empty orange juice glass stood in the sink. Just as she was beginning to think she was risking a lot for damned little, she noticed another door off the breakfast nook. Her instinct warned her she was short on time, that Kirk wasn't going to stay in the shower forever, but she'd already made her way to the door.

It led to a small, sunny study that overlooked a bed of flowers in the side yard. A huge, furry white cat was curled up in the In box, snoozing. He opened one eye at Sage's arrival, then promptly closed it. Her kind of cat. She pulled out the swivel chair, sat and began riffling through the contents of the big oak desk. Despite her growing uneasiness and the feeling that she'd better hurry, she had to admit to a certain exhilaration. There was nothing quite like snooping through the things of a man who didn't want to be found out. Jackson Kirk was a mystery, and she was compelled to unravel what made him tick—above and beyond, she realized with a jolt, any connection he might have with her grandfather.

No, that was crazy, she thought, and tried to tell herself she only wanted to know about the paintings, about what Bradford Killibrew and Jackson Kirk had in common, why they were at odds. And yet she knew herself better than that. Even if she'd washed her hands of Grandpa, she'd want to know more about the man upstairs in the shower. Grandpa only made snooping necessary. Without him, well, who knew? She and Jackson Kirk might have gotten off to a better start. But it was also true that without Grandpa she might never have met Jackson Kirk.

Not that she was entertaining any romantic fantasies about him! She just wanted to know him, that was all.

Or so she told herself.

But what she found made no sense, was incoherent when she tried to fit it all together into a whole. There were letters from television networks, environmentalists, economists, art collectors, actors and actresses, yachtsmen and one individual who seemed to have spent the last thirty years studying the population of various islands in the South Pacific. Sage only took time to skim the letters before plodding on through bills, receipts and postcards from places like Cameroon and the Seychelles.

Who the devil *was* Jackson Kirk? Apparently it wasn't a simple question. He wasn't an engineer, doctor, lawyer or Indian chief. He seemed to have money of his own from a trust or inheritance, and yet he also seemed to work, to want to and need to work. He appeared to be capable of earning an income as a yachtsman, a naturalist, a documentary producer, even a guide for adventurers. He might have been any, all or none of these. It was difficult to tell. Sage's own career was a bit eclectic—she was a guide, a camp director, a counselor, a ski instructor, whatever she felt like being. Yet all her "careers" involved the outdoors and Colorado. Jackson Kirk's seemed to involve the whole world.

One file would lead her off in one direction, another in a very different direction, but none mentioned Bradford Killibrew or his stolen paintings. There was nothing that suggested the man who had tried to steal her nonexistent forty thousand dollars was now operating or had ever operated outside the law or even standard ethical behavior.

So what did her grandfather have against him? She thought of the enticing violet eyes and the menacing scar and the sheer natural arrogance of the man. It wouldn't be difficult, she supposed, to come up with things to have against a man like that. She had her own list.

She shuddered involuntarily, thinking of his strong hands on her shoulders, his hot tongue on hers, but there was a warmth and thrill to the shudder that surprised and disconcerted her. After he'd thrown her out, could she still yearn for some kind of physical contact with him? She shook her head and reached down to open the bottom right-hand drawer.

A hand clamped down on her wrist. "Oh, dear," she breathed as she was hauled up out of the chair and against the solid hairy wall that was Jackson Kirk's chest. All he wore was one of those little terry-cloth towel things Velcro-ed around his slim waist. He was clean and freshly shaved, the fragrance of his light cologne clouding her senses.

"You were warned," he said in a low, husky voice, his hand still firmly around her wrist.

"I just came in for a paper and pen . . . to jot down my grandfather's license plate number. I memorized it as he shot off this morning, but I was afraid I'd forget it before I got back to the hotel. . . ."

It wasn't a very good lie but the best she could come up with under the circumstances. Still holding her wrist so that he kept her just inches from his chest, he reached over and snatched a scrap of paper and a pen from the top of his desk. Both were in plain view. Sage made a mental note to work on her spontaneous lying if she planned to stay in San Diego for very long, and smiled suddenly to herself. She wasn't even remotely intimidated—warning or no warning. She was just intensely alert and feeling very, very much alive.

"Here," he said threateningly, "write."

He still didn't let her go. She leaned over and wrote. Might as well see the lie through, she thought. Then she gave him a quick smile, folded the scrap in half and tucked it into her skirt pocket. "Thanks. Now if you'll just unhand me, I'll be on my way—"

"You're a liar, Sage Killibrew, and a damned poor one."

"So suspicious. Why don't you just call us even, all right? You tried to steal forty thousand dollars from me and all *I've* done is snoop in your office—allegedly. I deny it, of course."

"Of course."

There was a lilt to his voice now, a quiet amusement that she found more disturbing than the unadulterated anger. His grip on her wrist relaxed, and then, ever so slowly, he opened his hand and slid it up her forearm, massaging it in tiny, erotic circles.

"You don't lie often, do you?" he asked, his voice intimate and seductive, his eyes bright.

She shook her head, her throat tightening, but not with anything even resembling fear. With anticipation, she thought. With longing. She suddenly realized she didn't want to be anywhere else in the world but right here. "I haven't had to," she said.

"Consider yourself lucky. You're not married, are you?"

Good God. But she shook her head again. "No."

"Anyone who'll come looking for you if you don't return to Colorado right away?"

"No one big and ugly and mean, but I have friends. Why? Planning to pitch me over a cliff?"

He laughed, a slow, deep, guttural sound that seemed to go with the light touch of his fingers on her forearm. "Don't give me any ideas. Knowing you, you'd just sprout wings and fly back in my face. I was just wondering, that's all."

"I see." She didn't, wasn't sure she wanted to. "Well, I suppose I should be going."

She started to back away from him. What an act of will that was, she thought, just to walk away from the sensations he was arousing with his touch, with his mere presence, nearly naked, his hair damp, his chest and legs hard and muscular.

But she didn't get far. Jackson's smile stopped her. "Don't you want your punishment?" he asked.

"My *punishment*? Just who the hell do you think you are to dish out—"

"I asked if you wanted it, Sage. Myself, I'd hardly call it punishment. It's much more of a reward, I'd say—for being so predictably crazy, perhaps. And you do re-

member, don't you?" His eyes gleamed. "You *were* warned."

"But you weren't serious. You're not the type, Kirk, to haul a woman off to bed against her will."

"Exactly."

"Right. So there, I can leave."

He dropped his hand from her forearm and gestured toward the door. "Naturally. I won't stop you."

"Fine."

But she didn't move, not for that split second that told him she didn't want to leave. It was everything, it seemed, he needed, wanted, to know, and he stepped toward her. She breathed in his scent and felt her lips parting and her arms lifting as he slipped his under hers, sliding them around her waist and bringing her against him. His skin was cool. She opened her hands on his back and let her fingers soak up the feel of him, the hardness, the sensuality.

"This is crazy," she said.

He laughed softly, bringing his mouth toward hers. "Then it's right up your alley."

Her lips seemed to touch his first, just grazing them, and then her mouth opened and his tongue met hers. She moaned with longing, felt its deep pang inside her. Willingly she let Jackson press her against him. The skimpy towel might not have been there. She could feel his arousal and rubbed against it with the same primitive rhythm their kiss had taken on. He cupped her bottom with his hands and brought her harder against him, groaning into her mouth as his tongue circled hers, probing, inviting, arousing. She felt as if there was no stopping them. She wanted to tear her clothes off— wanted to have *him* tear her clothes off—and make love right there on the study floor.

But they both backed off, breathing raggedly, agonized with a longing they knew wouldn't be fulfilled. There was Grandpa Killibrew to consider, of course, and the paintings and the money and the simple fact that they hardly knew one another. Sexual attraction wasn't enough. There had to be more, and she sensed they both knew that.

To begin with, Sage thought, there had to be trust.

Jackson touched her cheek with the palm of his hand. He made no attempt to turn from her to conceal just how much she had aroused him but stood there close to her, bold and honest. It was a small gesture but something, and apparently the only one she would get.

"You'd better go," he said.

There would be no trust, not yet, perhaps not ever. If he trusted her, he would invite her to sit out on his terrace and drink iced lemonade and talk. If she trusted him, she'd invite herself.

Instead, she nodded, straightened her blouse and left without looking back.

EXCEPT FOR TRYING, unsuccessfully, to follow up on Grandpa's license plate number, Sage passed the rest of the afternoon as a tourist, relieved to be out of the hustle and bustle of her daily routine. She jogged on the beach, played tennis, went for a swim using a suit she picked up in a hotel shop, relaxed in the sun. And for the most part felt alone and frustrated. Her Plan B wasn't working. She knew little more than she had when she'd first arrived in San Diego, and only what her grandfather and his nemesis Jackson Kirk had deigned to tell her. It was more than frustrating, she thought; it was damned annoying.

Late in the afternoon she got into her rented car. As she drove past Jackson's street, she thumbed her nose, irritated with him now though still recalling in vivid detail all that had transpired earlier. Her first stop was a clothing store with southern California-type clothes in the window display. Splurging, she bought herself a couple of skirts and tops, some dressy sandals, a straw hat, two pairs of shorts and a dress. A perfect dress, if she did say so. It was periwinkle-blue knit and sleek, a great style for her tall frame, fancy enough for dinner at the Hotel Del, but not so fancy that she couldn't wear it with her new sandals. It was an extravagance considering she just might get fed up and leave San Diego in the morning, but she whipped out her credit card and paid the bill without batting an eye. She always told her teenage hikers to be prepared. Best, she thought, to follow one's own advice.

Laden with parcels, Sage wandered around and found a bookstore, where she left her things at the counter and, on a whim, made her way to the art section. Most of the books were on Renoir and Van Gogh and Michelangelo, but she found one devoted to contemporary art. Flipping to the index, she checked under *K*.

And there was the name Bradford Killibrew. She couldn't believe it! When he'd said he was a painter, she hadn't expected him actually to be listed in an art book. He was mentioned on pages seventy-nine and eighty, which Sage immediately turned to. A seascape resembling the one on Jackson's library wall was pictured, and the text discussed his work from a technical standpoint. Sage knew zilch about art but did figure out that her grandfather had turned the techniques and traditions of seascape painting on their heads, not so much tossing them out as rethinking and reworking them. While most widely known for his seascapes, he had also done a number of South American village scenes. The biographical notes were sketchy at best:

Although Killibrew has been painting since the 1960s, he has gained international attention only recently, beginning with his one-man show in Sao Paulo in 1983. Rumored to be in his seventies, Killibrew is reclusive and has never given an interview. It's not known where he makes his permanent home.

So Grandpa was just as elusive to the art world as he was to his family. Sage found that heartening from an emotional point of view, but not helpful as far as facts went. She checked the copyright date of the book—1986. Maybe he'd given up some of his privacy since then. Maybe a profile on him was about to appear in the *New York Times* and that was why he'd contacted Sage—he knew his family, although not art aficionados, did read the *Times*. At least Auntie and Juniper did, and perhaps even Summerfield. Sage didn't, and she doubted her father ever went to the trouble.

Of course, that didn't explain the forty thousand dollars or Jackson Kirk.

With a heavy sigh Sage replaced the expensive book on the shelf, bought a paperback thriller and headed back to the hotel. Nothing felt right. She didn't know what in blazes to do. Go back and talk to Jackson Kirk—*without* letting sparks start flying between them? That was illogical, she told herself. Why would he talk now just because she knew a little bit more about her grandfather? She had no leverage with Kirk and wasn't about to use the sexual attraction between them to get her way.

A, she probably wouldn't get her way, no matter what she did. B, she'd hate herself if she did get her way.

Sitting on the edge of her bed, she finally threw up her hands and called New Hampshire.

Her sister answered the phone. Sage smiled at the sound of Juniper's voice, happy and at peace with herself and the world, not to mention her family. "I'm not calling too late, am I?" Sage asked.

"Sage! I was just thinking about giving you a ring. Of course you're not calling too late. Cal and I just scraped off the last layer of wallpaper in the dining room and were about to celebrate with a bottle of champagne. How's Colorado?"

"You two could afford to pay someone to fix up that monstrosity of a house."

"But it wouldn't be as much fun. Strangers in the house would..." Sage could almost see her sister's sly grin. "Let's just say they'd hamper our style."

"I'll bet."

"So what's up?"

Sage hesitated. "I'm in San Diego."

"On vacation?"

"No, I—" She bit off a sigh. "I probably shouldn't be telling you this. He didn't ask me not to, but he didn't ask me to, either, and with the mess he's in, well, who knows *what* to do."

"Maybe just talking will help," Juniper said. "I'm all the way out here in Portsmouth, Sage, with a schedule that would fell a mule and a husband I've kind of grown attached to. If you think I'd interfere..."

"It's not so much that as... Oh, hell. Juniper, Grandpa Killibrew contacted me."

"*What!* I thought you were talking about a boyfriend! What do you mean, Grandpa Killibrew contacted you?"

Quickly and succinctly Sage related the events of the past week, leaving out only two rather extraordinary kisses. They were, she decided, superfluous to the main events. True to her nature, Juniper listened without interrupting.

"I'll be on the first plane out there," she said when Sage had finished.

"What about your schedule and your husband?"

"My schedule can wait, and Cal will understand."

"Juniper, I'd love to have you out here. You know that. But I'm not sure it's a good idea. Grandpa's already washed his hands of me, and this Kirk character won't tell me anything, either. I'm probably just wasting my time."

"Would it help if I wired you the forty thousand?"

"Probably not, at least not at this point. I think Grandpa relishes stealing the paintings."

Juniper groaned. "He could land up in jail!"

Sage hadn't considered that possibility, but Juniper's speculation could very well be true. Impulsive and plain mad as he was, Grandpa Killibrew could easily do something that would get him arrested.

"But they're his paintings," Sage pointed out.

"So *he* says."

"My God, that sounds like something Kirk would say."

"Maybe you should listen to him, then. Sage, you know what Grandpa's like. The best way to help him is to stop him from doing anything ridiculous. I know you're just as bullheaded and about as nuts as he is. I mean, honestly, going to San Diego with a briefcase full of Monopoly money! But at least you're coming at this from an objective standpoint. He's obviously emotionally involved."

"He called Kirk a fiend and a wretch."

"See?"

Sage leaned back against her pillows and looked out at the ocean view, as the vibrant colors of the sunset crept into the sky, reminding her of Jackson's eyes. Maybe she wasn't going at this problem from an objective standpoint, either. She said without relish, "So I'm supposed to be sensible and keep Grandpa out of trouble."

"If you can," Juniper replied. "I know it's a difficult task."

"For me, you mean."

"No, for anyone. Unless he's changed."

"He hasn't, not in that way."

"Is there anything I can do?"

"Apparently Grandpa's been making a name for himself as an artist. Maybe you and Cal can check with your various contacts—you know, all the big shots you hobnob with—and pull together some more facts for me. I'd like to find out who does have his paintings."

Juniper exhaled, saying nothing for a moment. Then she went on quietly, "It's hard to believe, isn't it? We could have tracked him down years ago, probably."

"If we'd only known where to look, but we didn't."

"And he didn't want us to."

"There's that."

"Okay, Sage, I'll find out what I can from Cal's and my 'big shot' friends."

"Thanks."

"Be careful, all right?"

Sage gave a fearless laugh. "Remember who you're talking to, June."

"I am," her sister replied gravely and, saying goodbye, hung up.

6

DRESSED IN A NEW skirt and top, Sage was drinking her first cup of coffee on the terrace when Jackson Kirk pulled out a chair opposite her and sat down. She had caught his figure moving along in the sunshine out of the corner of her eye but hadn't recognized him. Gone was any hint of the desperado. He wore casual natural linen pants, a white shirt and an unstructured jacket as violet and devil-may-care as his eyes. The effect left her breathless.

He gave her one of the half smiles that had warmed her dreams during the night and ordered coffee. "Good morning," he said.

She inclined her head in a polite but cool gesture, recalling their parting the day before. His behavior had been inexcusable, she'd decided. So had hers, but she'd already made peace with herself. She hadn't made any peace with Jackson Kirk. "Morning. What brings you here—besides the view, of course?"

"You."

"Ah-ha."

"Not in the sense you obviously think, so don't get that hunted look. I came to apologize. I haven't behaved especially well the past few days and I want you to know that I intend to reform. I don't ordinarily stalk women at seedy hotel bars and zoos, I don't steal and I don't lie. But I'm in a difficult situation and I—" he brought his coffee cup up to his lips and blew softly into it, his eyes searching hers across its rim "—I didn't realize I'd be dealing with someone like you."

She buttered a little piece of fresh, hot, exquisite Danish. "You forgot about the kisses."

"Ah, but there I'd be lying." He spoke with a delicious softness and honesty. "I can't apologize for kissing you because I don't regret it."

"And you do ordinarily kiss women, is that it?"

He drank some of his coffee and set the cup down, his eyes never leaving hers. "Only ones who are especially nutty and have huge round blue eyes."

"What's this?" she asked sharply, but she could hear the underlying amusement, the delight, even as she told herself she should resist the lure of his words. But who didn't like to have their eyes complimented? "Seems to me you've dug yourself out of one hole, and now you're about to dig yourself deeper into another."

He grinned. "Just being honest."

"Please."

"You're the one who asked—and if *you* were being honest, you'd admit those kisses weren't my doing alone."

She gave him a look that was meant to counter his statement, but, of course, she knew better. He was right. She *had* admitted as much—but only to herself. She wouldn't admit it to him, if only because she'd arrived at a Plan C: find Grandpa Killibrew and throw her lot in with him. Juniper was right. She couldn't leave that wild old man to his own devices, and Sage, of course, didn't want anything to happen to him, including imprisonment. So she had to present herself as an ally, find out who had his paintings, the circumstances under which they'd left his possession and how to get them back, legally and ethically.

And she didn't dare encourage Jackson Kirk, either by being too obstinate or too nice, to tag along. In her grandfather's eyes he was a fiend and a wretch, and Grandpa would only brand her a traitor if she even tried to find out otherwise. There'd be no chance to form an alliance, to help him.

And that, not Jackson Kirk, had to be her priority. Despite the longing she had sensed in him the day before, Sage was confident Jackson would survive her apparent rejection. Besides, maybe she was reading emotion into his words where there was none. Given his own proclivity for treachery, Jackson could just be fishing for information about her grandfather, anyway. Sexual desire still filled the air between them—there was no use pretending it didn't—but that was *all* there was between them. And Sage could handle that. She was, after all, a mature adult. She could keep her hormones from leading her down a path she knew she didn't want to follow.

But it was changing her mind about Jackson Kirk that worried her!

And, of course, she had no control over *his* hormones.

"Well, never mind," she told him briskly, "the rest of the apologies will do. We'll start with a fresh slate, okay? There, now. Surely I'm keeping you from something?"

"Are you always this obvious?"

"Subtlety isn't my long suit."

"You want me gone."

"Uh-huh."

"Is your grandfather on his way?"

She shook her head, biting into a buttery croissant. Luscious. The hell with Grandpa; maybe she'd just stay here all day and eat. "Not that I know of."

Jackson reached across the table and took a steaming muffin from her plate—a hand slapping offense, but she let him do it, anyway. "He won't tell you anything he doesn't want to, you know. He's a stubborn cuss."

"I may not have seen him for twenty years, but I do know what my grandfather's like." She was surprised by the defensiveness in her voice. Was she *jealous* because Jackson seemed to know her grandfather better than she did? "For someone who's known him only six months—"

"Forgot—that was one of my lies, Sage." He took a bite of muffin, looking relaxed and unconcerned, as if he, too, would like to sit there all day. "I've known Bradford Killibrew for ten years. As seems to run in the Killibrew family, he's stubborn, eccentric, independent and opinionated. He's also extraordinarily talented. The painting in my library, which I'm sure you examined as thoroughly as my study, is one of his. Nevertheless, I doubt he's listened to anyone in his entire life, and I don't expect he'll start now, least of all to me, and probably not to you."

"He used to listen to his wife," Sage said wistfully, remembering. "She was charming, beautiful, very wise. He left New Hampshire not long after her death. I think it galvanized him into leaving. Maybe they'd even discussed it before she died, and she encouraged him to pursue this dream of his to paint. Somehow—I don't know, maybe I'm wrong—but somehow I can't imagine him doing something quite so drastic without her support."

"I'd wondered," Jackson said, and Sage was pleased she knew something about Bradford Killibrew that he didn't know. "Bradford never spoke of her, of any of you, but I'd always guessed he'd had a past and people he cared about very deeply, all the more so because of his solitariness. He's not an easy man to understand."

"I know. Seeing him now, well, I can't imagine him being at the helm of Killibrew Traders any more than I can imagine myself being there. It just doesn't seem to suit him anymore. Has he been in San Diego all this time?"

"No, South America mostly—Brazil. He came to San Diego to get his paintings."

Sage started on her omelette, not wanting to say anything that would dissuade Jackson from talking. She felt herself opening up to him, not yet trusting him . . . but wanting to. Aching to. *Talk to me*, she thought. *Please talk to me. Tell me about my grandfather. Make it possible for something to happen between you and me.*

Not very productive thinking.

Jackson sighed, staring down at his coffee. "I don't know any of the details of what happened or why. We're both in the dark there, Sage. All I know is your grandfather needed some quick money, so he made a deal with a man who once was his closest friend." Jackson smiled sadly, picking at his muffin. "Now he refers to him as the devil himself. I don't know, maybe he's right. In any case, the deal involved four paintings. According to Bradford's understanding of their deal, he was to have been able to buy back the paintings for the same price he sold them."

"But this former friend won't sell them back now that Grandpa's a hot item," Sage suggested.

"I don't know if that's the reason, but he definitely won't sell them back. I even tried to buy them so *I* could sell them to Bradford, but that didn't work. I was found out, and I doubt Bradford would have taken them from me, anyway."

"Would you have let him pay with Monopoly money?"

Jackson smiled faintly. "I probably would have, but he never would have agreed. Your grandfather's a proud man. Now all he wants is revenge—or maybe only justice, I don't know."

"And you're caught in the middle."

A distant look came into his eyes. "More than you know."

"I suppose I am, too. Who's this former friend? Is it anyone I might know? An art dealer? Is he a friend of yours, too?"

Jackson didn't answer at once, and Sage didn't push him, watching as he finished his muffin and drank his coffee and then stared impassively out to sea. She was drawn to this pensive side of him as much as to the angry "desperado" who'd pushed himself at her in the Happy Trails lounge.

At length he said, "His name's Reuben Kirk."

Sage winced. "Oh, dear."

"My father."

"Then your loyalties must be torn."

"Until I learn the facts, I'm trying to remain neutral. I don't know enough details to make any judgments. But I know my father—and I know your grandfather. They've done a complete about face; they loathe each other. I won't even predict what they might try to do." He paused, looking up at her with such warmth she could feel her bones begin to melt. "Help me stop them, Sage. Bradford's undoubtedly got himself another scheme, but he'd never let me in on it, not now. If you could find out what he's up to, buy me some time so I can negotiate a peaceful solution—"

"*You wretched fiend!*"

They both swung around at the sound of Bradford Killibrew's bellow. Wretched fiend? Sage wondered how she could take any of this seriously with such histrionics, but then realized that they were at the elegant Hotel del Coronado, not the Happy Trails. Grandpa probably thought he was being civilized.

"I think I'd better make my exit," Jackson said in a low voice. "I'll be in touch."

Sage set down her fork. "I'm not making any promises. Until *I* know the facts, I have to be on my grandfather's side. I don't think I can be neutral."

In his baggy chinos and a flour-sack shirt, Grandpa swooped over to her table. "You're one sorry individual, Kirk," he sneered, his face reddening as he raised one fist. "You're as bad as your father. Maybe even worse. I ought to have had you arrested for breaking into my boat! Maybe that would have kept you out of my way."

"I only did that as a last resort to find out what you were up to."

"That's how you found out about Sage and the money."

"Of course, but I was only trying to prevent the two of you from doing something that was bound to backfire. You know as well as I do that even if you had the money, my father isn't going to sell you back your paintings."

Grandpa snorted, both fists raised now. "I was going to shove the money up his nose and *take* my paintings."

"Exactly what I was afraid of." Jackson rose calmly. "As I said, you wouldn't listen to reason."

"Damned right. 'Reason' only makes matters worse."

"Wait a minute," Sage said, "both of you. Why don't we all sit down and talk this over? Maybe we can..."

Grandpa shot her a look. "I've done all the talking I intend to do."

It was a polite way of telling her to shut her mouth and mind her own damned business. She shut her mouth, but her mind kept working.

Unlike Sage, Jackson knew when to quit. "I think Mother was right: I shouldn't even bother with you two. If you kill each other or both land up in jail, it'll be nobody's fault but your own. Stew in your own juice, Bradford." He turned to Sage, his features softening slightly, his eyes flickering with promise and hope. "Thanks for the coffee."

She would have watched his tall figure amble across the terrace, but Grandpa blocked her view as he shoved aside Jackson's coffee cup with a belligerent grunt and sat down. "He's not to be trusted, you know that?"

"I don't *know* anything," she said irritably. "Grandpa, what are you doing here? I thought you wanted me back in Colorado and were putting Plan B into operation."

He shrugged. "I need a hand. You, unless you've thrown your lot in with Kirk."

"I haven't thrown my lot in with anyone. Do you want something to eat?"

"Looks pretty good," he said, peering across the table at her plate. "Sure, why not?"

Sage ordered some fresh coffee, and had Grandpa load a plate with muffins and pastries at the buffet table. His troubles apparently hadn't affected his appetite. She sipped her coffee, wishing Jackson hadn't made such a quick retreat. She'd have liked to know more about his escapade on her grandfather's boat. That, she noted, hadn't appeared on his apology list or in his explanation of precisely what he did and didn't know. Obviously he hadn't told her everything. She didn't feel betrayed, only a baby step ahead of him. Much better, she thought, than feeling as if he was tromping all over her.

As soon as Grandpa was safely into his second Danish, Sage said, "Jackson told me you and his father were in some kind of blood feud."

His beady old eyes popped out at her. "Jackson, is it now?"

"Grandpa, please."

"Reuben Kirk makes his son look like the Archangel Gabriel, which is saying something, given my opinion of the man."

"The wretched fiend," Sage said with a straight face.

Bradford Killibrew nodded in solemn agreement. "We made a deal, Reuben and I, about eighteen, twenty months ago. I kept up my end, he didn't keep up his."

"Something to do with some of your paintings."

"Four paintings—two seascapes, two village scenes. I sold them to him."

"Oh, dear." She'd been hoping Jackson had been wrong about that part.

Grandpa held up a hand, silencing her protest. "Under certain conditions, which he agreed to."

"You have a contract?"

"Good heavens, woman, you sound like your sister. Of course not. It was a handshake deal, between gentlemen and friends. He was to sell them back to me for the price he paid when I saw fit."

"And he changed his mind?"

"That he did."

"Because their market value has increased?"

Grandpa waved his fork. "I sold them below market value as it was."

"And you a successful Yankee businessman, a veritable legend in your time. Grandpa, I have no sympathy for you. If you didn't know better, that would be one thing, but my God, you *founded* Killibrew Traders, one of the most successful catalog clothing companies of its kind! Now look at you—mooching meals off your granddaughter, skulking about in baggy old chinos, driving a rattletrap of a car, living on a boat. That *is* where you live, isn't it, on your boat?"

He scoffed at her as he buttered a muffin. "If I'd wanted a lecture, I'd have sailed up to Portsmouth and gotten myself one from your Auntie Killibrew, who happens to be the best at it. Now don't talk about things you don't know a damned thing about. Reuben Kirk and I were *friends*. Even thirty years ago when Traders was just beginning to catch on, friendship meant something to me. It's become to mean even more since I gave up the company. Unfortunately, it doesn't mean a blessed thing to Reuben."

Sage sighed, wishing her grandfather had something more tangible to stand on than principle. "So Reuben Kirk reneged on a handshake deal and won't sell you back the paintings. Morally, you probably have every right to be outraged. Legally—legally, Grandpa, you're probably stuck."

"I know that," he snapped. "Why do you think I plan to steal the damned things?"

"But I thought that was Plan B."

"I've incorporated it into Plan C. Problem with Plan B is it's based on my knowing where Reuben's got the paintings stashed; I don't. That's where you come in."

Sage wasn't sure she wanted to comment. She broke off a bit of her last muffin and swallowed it with coffee.

"This younger devil obviously has an eye for you," Grandpa went on, slathering butter on a muffin. "You can find out from him where his father's got my paintings."

"Then tell you."

"Of course. So I can make my plans."

"To steal them."

"To force the old scoundrel to keep his end of our deal."

Juniper was right: Grandpa *could* end up in jail. "I'm not sure I want to do that."

He swallowed and paused long enough to give her a short, probing look. "Gotten to you, has he?"

"No, that's not it at all. Grandpa, maybe we should try to be sensible."

"Parading around the Happy Trails Hotel with a briefcase reputedly filled with forty thousand dollars in cash was sensible?" He snorted, setting down his fork and wiping his mouth with his napkin. "Trust me, Sage. I won't get you into any serious trouble."

She supposed he considered Jackson Kirk "minor" trouble; she wished she could agree. "It's not that, it's, well, if this Reuben Kirk is as bad as you say, he could have you arrested."

Grandpa grinned. "First, Sage m'dear, he's got to catch me."

End of discussion. He emptied his plate, drank two more cups of coffee and refused to answer any more questions—including where he had his boat docked—commenting only on the view and its peculiar mingling of light, air and water. Then, as he left, saying he'd contact her again soon, he remarked on the color of Jackson's jacket. "Violet, wasn't it?" He shook his head and chuckled. "Like to see *that* one on the pages of a Killibrew Traders catalog!"

And off he went, still chuckling to himself.

THERE WAS NO LISTING for Reuben Kirk in Sage's trusty telephone book, but something about the name nagged her. It sounded familiar, a name she knew but hadn't placed in the right context. Was he also an artist? A renowned collector? A gangster? She muttered in disgust as she shut the phone book. At this point *anything* seemed possible.

She had no desire to wait around the hotel all day for one party or another in this mess to come and tell her another few facts. She'd go nuts. Instead, she grabbed her bag and headed out. Might as well go find trouble as wait for it to find her.

Jackson Kirk was climbing into his Alfa Romeo as she passed his house, and she quickly headed down another street, turned around and doubled back. How convenient, she thought. This was her first stroke of luck—unless, of course, he was just going to the grocery store. Or to a lover's. Kisses or no kisses, she had no reason to believe she was the only woman in his life. Or even *a* woman in his life. And she told herself she didn't want to be. It was all too complicated, too soon.

Glad her car wasn't noticeable and his was, she followed Jackson over the sweeping Bay Bridge to San Diego, then north on the freeway to La Jolla. When he got off the freeway in the exclusive seaside community, he headed toward the ocean. Traffic thinned. Sage followed at a discreet distance, and when he turned into the driveway of a plushly landscaped house tucked on a hill overlooking the Pacific, she memorized the address and drove right past it. She wandered around La Jolla for thirty minutes, then doubled back.

She parked down the street around a bend and walked up to the house. It was quite a place—spacious, quiet, the sloping grounds filled with light and color. Although it was fenced off by wrought iron, it didn't have the look or feel of a fortress. Sage wasn't sure whether she should march up to the front door and announce herself or sneak around for a while.

Sneak around, she decided. If this wasn't Reuben Kirk's house, then she could make a discreet retreat without having made a fool of herself.

She went through the front gate and immediately veered off the walkway onto the carefully tended lawn, lush and green at this time of year. The light fragrance of the flowers and greenery mingled with the stronger smell of the ocean, and she had a sudden vision of herself lying in a hammock somewhere, reading a book. Life could be worse. Shoving aside such absurd fantasies, she wound her way under the bougainvillea to the back of the house.

A swimming pool glittered, blue and inviting, in the early afternoon sun. Two men sat at a limestone-topped table, on leather chairs with wooden lattice bases. One was Jackson, as breathtaking as ever. The other was a thinner man, just as tall, his white hair sprinkled with a few dark strands. He radiated a kind of kinetic energy that Sage could feel even at a distance . . . and she suddenly realized who he was.

Reuben Kirk. *Of course.* The film director and, more and more in recent years, producer. As she recalled, he'd won an Academy Award for a film set in South America, in Brazil. Where Grandpa spent a lot of time.

So that was the devil himself. The man who had somehow snookered Bradford Killibrew out of four paintings. Sage felt herself tilting even more toward her grandfather's side. Reuben Kirk didn't need to rob a nearly impoverished artist. And rob *was* the word. He could easily afford to pay the going rate for Grandpa's paintings—not that Grandpa would give him that chance. If Reuben Kirk had proven to be in as dubious financial circumstances as her grandfather, Sage might have reserved judgment. But he was clearly rich, and no matter how naive Grandpa had been to sell him the paintings on a handshake deal, Reuben Kirk had no moral justification for keeping them. He couldn't.

Now, for sure, Sage was on her grandfather's side, wholly and completely. One hundred percent. As she watched the elder Kirk gesture wildly, impatience in his every move, she decided *she'd* steal the damned paintings herself, if it came to that. The man was a shark who'd taken advantage of a friend. How could she be neutral!

Juniper would say her younger sister was acting impulsively, jumping to conclusions before all the facts were in, but Sage didn't care. Grandpa had *trusted* this man— only to be double-crossed.

She refused to think about Jackson or to even look at him. He only confused matters. Ducking under a huge bougainvillea, she made her way back around to the front of the house. If those two were occupied out back, there was a good chance she could slip inside and have a look around. Maybe find the paintings. Maybe even have the opportunity to sneak them out and have this whole mess over and done with. Reuben Kirk could collect the insurance or take a loss. She didn't care.

But as she stepped lightly, silently, onto the walkway, she heard a rustle behind her. A cat, a snake... She whirled around, ready to act.

"I was wondering when you'd show up."

"Jackson." She groaned, and for some dumb reason noticed that he'd taken off his violet jacket. It didn't matter. His eyes still gleamed, catching the flickering light, throwing her senses into a tizzy. Obviously a discreet retreat was impossible now. A quick one, however, was clearly in order. She said, "Nice to see you" and bolted.

One muscular arm sliced around her waist from behind and hauled her up off the ground, then hard against him. She considered kicking him in the shins, or somewhere higher, but reconsidered when his grip slackened ever so slightly and he whispered into her ear, "Don't even *think* you might get away with it."

"With what?" She tried to turn to show him the feigned look of innocence in her eyes but found she couldn't. He had her nicely pinned against him. Maybe, she thought, she didn't want to find an escape.

"You know perfectly well what. You may be a mountain woman, but I assure you, I'm just irritated enough to—"

"Think you're tough, don't you? I could scream and alert your father."

Jackson laughed, his breath tickling her ear. "You'd be lucky if the least he did was have you arrested for trespassing. You're as bad as your grandfather."

She glanced down at the tensed arm around her waist. Her arms were free, which meant he wasn't too serious about hanging on to her—unless, of course, he didn't realize what being a "mountain woman" had taught her about self-preservation. "If you'll let me go," she said, giving him one last shot at being reasonable, "I'll consider giving you an explanation."

"You'll explain whether or not I let you go."

Obviously "reasonable" wasn't in his present code of conduct. Still, she couldn't feel anything approaching outrage. Discomfort, yes; embarrassment, a little. But not anger. In fact, she was suppressing a mad urge to massage his arm the way he had hers when he'd caught her snooping in his study.

"If you want to threaten me, Kirk," she said, "you have to make me believe you'll follow through. Now, just exactly what will happen if I don't cooperate?"

His arm slipped lower, his fingers tracing erotic patterns just above her hip. "I'll make mad passionate love to you right here under the damned bougainvillea."

"You think so, huh?"

"I know so." Pressing her harder against him, he flicked his tongue against her ear, then trailed wet, hot kisses down her neck. "Believe me, I know so."

All at once Sage was quaking with longing, and every fiber of her body begged her just to lie down under the bougainvillea and make love to the man. "You're definitely one of Auntie's rogues," she said but couldn't tell whether she'd spoken aloud or not, she was so preoccupied with the tingling sensations, the wonderful ache all over her body.

"One of who's what?"

"Enough's enough, Jackson."

"I don't think we'll ever get enough of each other," he whispered, his voice raspy.

To prove his point, he rubbed against her bottom, and she could feel his arousal, which further inflamed her, making what she had to do more difficult, more regrettable.

"I guess I must bring out the caveman in you or something." She tried to sound nonchalant, but even she heard the passion-choked sound of her voice.

"Mmm," he murmured, tracing the outside of her ear with his tongue. "You bring out everything in me. You're crazy, you're beautiful, you're—"

"Jackson, we *can't*."

He straightened, stopped kissing her, stopped arousing her with the light touch of his fingers. The muscles in the arm around her hardened again. "For a minute there I'd forgotten the point of all this," he said. "Care to explain what you're doing here?"

"No, I don't."

And with that enough *was* enough. She shoved both her elbows into his chest, with just enough force to surprise him, which she did. His grip loosened, and she darted off, ducking under the bougainvillea and making a beeline for the street.

He knew the grounds better than she did, however, and when she tripped over a jade plant, he was there when she hit the grass. As she scrambled to her feet, he caught her around the knees, flipped her over and jumped on top of her.

They were eye to eye. She let her head fall back in the soft grass and laughed up at the sky. "You wretch," she said, loving the feel of his chest heaving against hers. "*Now* what?"

He grinned down at her. "You tell me."

But a shadow fell over them, and they both looked up at the frowning, angular face of Reuben Kirk. "Do you mind telling me," he said in a curiously calm, cultured voice, "what in blazes is going on here?"

7

"LET ME HANDLE THIS," Jackson said.

Sage peered around him at the bewildered man standing above them. Reuben Kirk looked none too pleased to find his son wrestling a strange woman in his yard, and Sage was perfectly willing to turn this one over to Jackson. "Gladly," she said.

Jackson rolled off her onto the grass and sat close to her, with his hands flat behind him, elbows straightened, knees bent. He didn't look at all embarrassed. Realizing her skirt was halfway up her thighs, Sage quickly shoved it back down and sat up, picking a blade of grass from her hair. At least making love under the bougainvillea was out, she thought, fighting a mad urge to giggle. She felt like a teenager caught necking out on the front porch.

"Who's this?" Reuben Kirk demanded of his son, with an imperious nod at Sage. "What's going on here?"

Jackson remained composed. "Father, I'd like you to meet a friend of mine. Sage," he said blandly; she was grateful he hadn't used her last name. It wasn't the appropriate moment to confront Reuben Kirk with her identity as a Killibrew. Jackson went on, "Sage, this is my father, Reuben Kirk."

"How do you do," Sage greeted him politely, wondering if it would be better or worse if she got up from the grass.

Reuben Kirk grunted something about being pleased to meet her, but his piercing gray-blue eyes were studying her altogether too closely. He shared his son's ability to look menacing. "Haven't we met before?"

Sage grimaced in discomfort: it was her "spitting image" resemblance to Grandpa Killibrew, damn his beady eyes. "I don't think so. I'm sure I'd remember." She decided to change the subject—quickly. "I admire your work, Mr. Kirk."

"Thank you." He continued to look suspicious.

"I'd asked Sage to meet me here," Jackson said, rising and brushing himself off. Sage admired him for looking so unruffled under the circumstances. "I'm afraid she tripped on her way to find me."

The frown disappeared from the elder Kirk's hard-bitten, tanned face, and something approaching warmth, even amusement, came into his eyes. Perhaps the man had a mercurial nature, but so did Grandpa, and suddenly Sage could see them as friends. "I see."

Sage was afraid he did. She managed a smile as she rose, somewhat indelicately but with speed. Her sleuthing had ended in ignominy. She couldn't wait to be gone. "Clumsy of me, I know."

"We were just leaving," Jackson said, taking her by the elbow. "I was wondering if I might bring her to dinner tomorrow evening? Would that be convenient?"

Dinner? What was the man up to? Was he crazy? Whose side was he on? Sage had a sudden urge to march past both him and his father and fetch her grandfather's paintings. *Then* they could discuss having dinner together!

"Certainly," Reuben Kirk said, all the warmth vanishing from his eyes. He knew something was up. He looked at Sage, very cool, very probing. Sage met his gaze head-on. He said to her, "I apologize if my grounds caused you any... confusion."

She shrugged. "It's my new sandals—they're slippery."

"I understand. Well, it's a pleasure, Sage. Dinner's at eight, but we'll be gathering for cocktails at seven. I'll see you then."

He ambled off, regal and very much in control, and seeming not at all to be the kind of man to abscond with someone's paintings. Just what he'd figured out, even what he guessed, she couldn't say, and wasn't sure she wanted to know. She turned to Jackson. "Dinner?" she fumed. "*Dinner?*"

His expression was impossible to read. "You came here to find the paintings, didn't you?"

"Well..."

"Of course you did, probably so you can report back to your grandfather and he can proceed with plans to steal them or whatever. God, you two."

"You're no better," she shot back. "Who broke into his boat?"

"An act of desperation."

"And what do you think this is?"

"An act of pure stubbornness."

"I prefer to think of it as justice." She tossed her head in a haughty gesture that probably wasn't very convincing. Haughty she definitely wasn't. What she wanted to do was stick her tongue out at him, to be juvenile and hotheaded, but that would undoubtedly only remind him of unfinished business. This was not the time to end up rolling in the grass! With a slight catch in her voice she asked, "Will I have a chance to see the paintings tomorrow night?"

"I think so. That's my father's plan, at any rate, but he's been so hard to read lately. There's no telling what he'll actually do."

"Then I'll definitely be here."

"With *me*, and dammit, you'll behave. If you try to steal the damned things, or if your grandfather shows up..."

She snorted. "I've had about all the threats I can handle!"

He took her by the shoulders and turned her toward him, not ungently. "I'm trusting you, Sage," he said, with a new and different note of seriousness—one that portended intimacy, frankness, long talks by the fireside. "Tomorrow night is for us. Unless your grandfather told you everything—and that I doubt, he being as close-mouthed as he is—you don't have any more idea of what the hell's going on between him and my father than I do."

She wasn't sure she wanted to see the hope and honesty that had come into his face, not now, not when so much else remained unclear and unresolved—like four Bradford Killibrew paintings. "Your father reneged on a deal they made about the paintings."

"So Bradford Killibrew says. My father says *Bradford* reneged."

"Oh, dear."

"Reserve judgment, Sage. Remain neutral until we find out more."

"I'm not sure I can."

He nodded, appreciating her frankness. "Then at least let tomorrow night be for us."

"What you mean is for me not to tell Grandpa I'm having dinner with your father."

"That's right," he admitted with that tantalizing half smile.

She hesitated. If she saw Grandpa between now and then, she'd tell him about the dinner. She'd have to. Finally she said, "I don't want to make a promise I can't keep, but I'll do what I can to keep tomorrow night peaceful. I won't do anything hasty."

"But you can't guarantee anything about your grandfather, if he somehow finds out. I understand. There's no telling what my father will do, either." He paused, thinking the matter over, then nodded. "It's a deal."

"Shake?"

He grinned devilishly. "Not a chance."

And their deal was sealed with a kiss, hard and quick and utterly delicious. She patted him on the cheek and lightly brushed his lips. "Till tomorrow night."

SAGE USED the rest of Sunday and most of Monday to regain her perspective on what was going on. She wanted to help Grandpa Killibrew, that much she knew. She wanted to get him out of trouble with Reuben Kirk—or Reuben Kirk out of trouble with Grandpa, whatever the case—and she wanted to know more about his art, his life during the past twenty years. She wanted the rest of the family to see him.

All that was enough, she realized, to bite off at one time. The exploding sexual tension between her and Jackson, well, that was just too much. She couldn't deal with that right now. She *shouldn't*. Her first priority should be her grandfather. And second priority, if she was being sensible, should be getting herself back to her life and work in Colorado.

"Jackson Kirk should be a—what?" she asked herself aloud, sitting out at the pool with her straw hat on and a glass of iced lemonade at her side. This caper did have its perks.

She scowled to herself. Jackson was just there to be dealt with, a presence rather than a priority. A hell of a noticeable presence, too. "He should behave himself, is what," she muttered.

And so should she. Which she would, she promised herself. Dinner tonight with the Kirks would be strictly business. She'd see to it there'd be no opportunity for hot kisses and sexy grins and goading that only served to ignite the sparks that flew between them. She wouldn't make any advances, give him any openings, and if he did, she would ignore them.

It was so much easier, of course, to be disciplined when he wasn't around.

When she headed up to her room, there was a message waiting from Juniper. "Sage: Bradford Killibrew's last painting sold for more than a hundred thousand dollars this spring. What's he do with his money? Juniper."

A damned good question!

Sage flopped onto her double bed, the drapes open and the sunlight streaming in. "A hundred grand!" she grumbled. "That old goat ought to be buying *me* breakfast!"

She wished there was some way of getting in touch with him, but checking his license plate had produced no results and there were more damned places than she could count to dock a boat in San Diego. She'd considered asking Jackson, but that would require calling him, having him come over, going over to his house: hearing his voice at best; at worst, seeing him. Neither prospect appealed to her. Or, to be more accurate, both appealed to her too much. She wasn't yet convinced she had steeled herself against his attractions.

So she took a shower and did her nails—given her "mountain woman" life-style, hardly a regular occurrence. She'd chosen a pale, pale pink polish. When she held her hands up to admire them, she thought they didn't look bad at all, and then her treacherous imagination floated images across her mind of her painted nails running through Jackson's dark hair, trailing lightly down his browned back.

The telephone rang, startling her out of her renegade fantasy. If it were Jackson, there was no telling what she'd do. Tell him to come on over, maybe and—No! She grabbed the phone, and the raspy voice of her grandfather responded to her greeting. "Find out anything?" he asked.

She rested against the headboard and tried to keep from smudging her not quite dry nails. "I found out your last painting sold for over a hundred thousand dollars," she said coolly. "That's a lot of money, Grandpa."

"You should see all the people who take their cut of it, too."

"It's still a lot of money."

"Bah, who needs money?"

"*You* do."

"I guess I am running a little short. But that's not why I want my paintings back from that old crook. Those particular ones I never had any intention of selling, which he damn well knows."

"But you did sell them."

"I think of it more as collateral for a loan I was ready to repay, as agreed."

There was an echo in his words of the Yankee businessman he'd once been. "Well, it doesn't make any difference," Sage said. "If you have money or access to money through your work, why on earth did you need to involve me?"

"I don't have any cash," he said. "Spent it. And I don't have any paintings I care to sell right now. Besides, that's not the point. Reuben Kirk stole my paintings, and I intend to steal them back. Now, do you have anything to report?"

She hesitated, wondering how much to tell him about yesterday—or tonight. She'd promised Jackson, and she had to admit she didn't want her grandfather barreling in before she'd had a chance to figure out what was going on. "I may have a lead on the paintings," she said carefully. "Let me emphasize may."

"Tell me."

"I can't. I have to protect my sources."

He snorted. "Your Jackson fellow, you mean?"

"Grandpa . . ."

"Don't trust him. He's as bad as his father."

"Grandpa, you asked for my help. I suggest you take what you get."

"Starchy thing, aren't you?" But she could hear the grudging approval in his voice. "When do you think you'll have something concrete?"

"Maybe tomorrow. I'll need to be able to reach you."

He didn't respond at once. Finally, reluctantly, he said, "I've moved the boat since Jackson broke in."

"I can't blame you," Sage said.

"I'm at a marina in La Jolla. It's expensive, but this way I'm close to the fiend Reuben and my paintings. I don't have a car anymore. The one I drove the other day I'd borrowed from a friend. Had to return it."

"That's all right. I'll come to you."

He gave her the name of the marina, and she promised on pain of all kinds of horrible things not to mention it to either Kirk. "Grandpa," she said, feeling again her attachment to this eccentric individual, "trust me, okay? I'm on your side."

"Tell that to your hormones," he said with a snort and hung up.

THEY ALMOST DIDN'T make it to dinner. Jackson arrived in her room promptly at six-thirty, devastating in tan linen. Every time she saw him, he seemed sexier than the last time, which was something since she'd thought him positively mouth-watering the moment he'd burst through those swinging doors at the Happy Trails. The scar, the incredible eyes, the fit body, the sheer unpredictability of the man combined to heighten her senses and fire her imagination...and, as Grandpa had pointed out, her hormones.

She remembered her vow to herself: she *wouldn't* be tempted.

For the evening she wore her new periwinkle dress, sandals, stockings she'd dashed out for at the last minute and her pink nails, of course. She'd spent all of fifteen minutes, three times her usual allotment, applying her cosmetics so they blended with her complexion, highlighting her natural glow. Her hair was as impossible as ever to control. She'd fiddled with it for a while, then decided to let it do as it pleased. But it was clean and shiny, and if she hadn't known better, she might have spent hours in a salon to get it to look so perfectly tousled.

Grabbing her handbag, she asked casually, "Am I underdressed? Grandpa's telegram certainly didn't prepare me for dinner with a famous movie producer."

"Underdressed?" Jackson laughed softly, moving toward her as his eyes roved over her. "Darlin', I'd say you were overdressed."

Before she could say anything, his arm circled her and his mouth found hers. Actually, she thought vaguely, reveling in his taste, she could have said something before he made contact—if she'd wanted to. There was time, opportunity, even now. All she had to do was pull away and say no. But, vow or no vow, she didn't want to. She wanted to taste his tongue, which she did, and trace the edges of his teeth, which she did, and feel herself sinking under the crushing weight of the sensation of being near him, touching him, arousing him.

He opened his hands at her sides and slid them up the close-fitting bodice of her dress until his thumbs were just below her breasts. She could feel her nipples harden inside her bra. He touched them, pressed them erotically, feeling their hardness, too. She moaned, backing up toward the bed.

"You know I want you," he whispered.

"And me you. Jackson . . ."

They kissed again, and all she wanted to do was strip off her clothes and lie naked beneath him, to feel his thrusts inside her, to rock with him, love with him, ache with him. How could this have happened so suddenly? How could she feel like this? How could she forget the repeated vows she'd made to herself to avoid just this?

"We'd better go," she choked out.

He pulled away, and she was gratified by his reluctance and the signs of arousal in his every move. "I know."

In his car she reapplied her lipstick on her passion-swollen lips and tried not to see in her reflection in the mirror the indication of how much she wanted him . . . and would go on wanting him.

"Did you promise to yourself that wouldn't happen?" she asked him.

He looked straight ahead. "Yes. You?"

"Mmm." She grinned. "We're terrible, aren't we?"

He gave her a dry look. "I'd say we lack a certain amount of willpower when in one another's presence."

"Do you? *I'd* say we just demonstrated tremendous willpower. I mean, there we were, there was the bed, there was the door to lock."

He put on the brakes and turned to her. "Shall we go back?"

"No! Good heavens, I'm feeling practically saintly. Don't tempt me further."

With a laugh he shifted into gear and headed out toward the Bay Bridge, which offered a panoramic view of downtown San Diego. "Is it just sex between us?" he asked.

"I'm not sure. I suppose I don't know you well enough even to answer. I'd . . . I guess I'd like to think not." She shrugged. "You're not a bad sort, you know. Interesting, at least. I find myself asking questions about you I can't answer—maybe even don't want to answer."

"And you're a nut," he said affectionately. "Crazy and irresistible. I like what I know about you—and I want to know more."

"This afternoon, during my swim, while I was supposed to be talking myself out of wanting to have anything to do with you, I envisioned us having long talks on an isolated beach or mountaintop—anywhere we could be alone without complications."

"Like two ornery old men?"

"For starters."

"We argue a lot, you know."

"Don't see eye to eye on much of anything, it seems."

"I suppose there'll always be complications."

"The question is," she said, looking out her window instead of at him, "will they always matter?"

The question remained unanswered, was perhaps unanswerable, and they drove the rest of the way to La Jolla in silence.

First priority: Grandpa, Sage repeated to herself, like a litany.

Second priority: back home to Colorado.

What about me? she asked silently. *Where do I fit in? Aren't I a priority?*

Of course, her inner voice replied, stern and uncompromising. *Your priorities arose out of your concern for yourself as well as others.*

No, they didn't. They arose out of fear.

And her inner voice asked, *What are you afraid of?*

Sage looked at Jackson, his striking face kissed by the setting sun. "I don't know," she murmured, and even he didn't hear her.

But her inner voice did, and this time it didn't offer an answer. Perhaps, she thought, because there wasn't one.

8

THE INTERIOR of Reuben Kirk's home was just as impressive as its grounds, exquisite and elegant, but somehow warm, as well—as contradictory, it seemed, as the man himself. Jackson had declined to discuss his father, telling Sage he preferred her to draw her own conclusions, and she found herself wondering what kind of childhood Jackson had had, what influence the elder Kirk had had on his son. There were no siblings, and his parents apparently had divorced. Sage, with her eccentric parents, had had a rather extraordinary childhood, but she couldn't imagine what it meant to have a father who'd won an Academy Award. Bad enough to have friends who wore Killibrew Traders clothes! She wondered if his father's fame had led Jackson to choose an existence out of the limelight in a little house in Coronado.

In any case, Reuben Kirk had only come to La Jolla recently. Probably, she thought, to escape the wrath of Bradford Killibrew.

The elder Kirk greeted Sage cordially but with reserve, and as Jackson led her to the dining room, she asked, "Do you think he suspects who I am?"

"I wouldn't be surprised. You look just like your grandfather. Just try not to act like him. And don't give me that innocent look. You know damned well you two have a hell of a lot more in common than just the color of your eyes."

Sage sniffed. "My sister, Juniper, says Grandpa's eccentric and irresponsibly impulsive."

"I rest my case," he said with a humorless smile.

They entered the dining room, a huge room done in neutral tones, one windowed wall overlooking the gardens and pool. The art on the other walls didn't resemble the seascape hanging in Jackson's library.

"You should talk," she said. "Who dressed up like some murderous gunslinger out of the Old West and tried to intimidate me into giving up my briefcase? Who tried to *steal* my briefcase? Who attacked me under the bougainvillea?" She stopped herself suddenly as she noticed desire coming into his eyes. "No, never mind, don't answer. Your father's place is really lovely. Not what I expected."

Jackson got two martinis from the bar and handed her one. "What did you expect?"

"I don't know. Something more—" she hunted for the right word "—Hollywood, I guess."

"Father tries to distance himself from the glitz and glitter of his profession—something he and your grandfather have in common. He's always spent a great deal of time in Brazil. He sold his California residence last year and planned to live permanently in South America, but that didn't work out. He says this place is only temporary, but I don't know, I think he likes it."

Sage tasted her martini as they wandered out to the gardens; it was potent. Reminding herself that Jackson would be driving her back to her hotel, she decided to limit herself to one. "Where does your mother live?"

"San Francisco. Father remarried last year, but the marriage didn't take," Jackson said. "They've divorced."

"Oh. I'm sorry."

"It's for the best, I think. She's a Brazilian—Ana Luiza Dantas—much younger than my father. They had absolutely nothing in common. Unfortunately, she saw that before he did and was the one to leave. He's still licking his wounds."

Sage nodded sympathetically. "So my grandfather's a convenient target for his anger. Their feud probably takes his mind off his personal pain."

"It's a point I've considered. Father denies it, however."

"He sounds as immovable as Grandpa."

"Their friendship has always been incredibly volatile."

They walked among the flowers and greenery, and then along the terrace by the pool, mingling with guests, talking of nothing more serious than the colors of the sunset. Sage felt curiously at ease. When dinner was served, she sat next to Jackson. Reuben Kirk sat at the head of the table, and Sage was struck by how alone he seemed. With all his fame and fortune he seemed to have so little of what mattered and he seemed to know it. She felt a sudden empathy for him. Perhaps, in his pain, he'd alienated a good friend and now was looking for a way to both save his dignity and restore their friendship. Sage wondered if she could persuade her grandfather to try negotiating a settlement, or at least let her or Jackson try.

But of course Grandpa didn't want a "settlement." He wanted his paintings, and she could easily be reading qualities into Reuben Kirk that weren't there. Her duty tonight was to discover where Grandpa's paintings were, to "case" the place, like a jewel thief. Her and Cary Grant, she thought, both drawn to the task and repelled by it.

Dinner was luscious, much more so than the frozen things she sometimes prepared on late dark nights in the mountains. Usually, though, she'd just cook a chicken or something on Sunday and eat it all week. And then there were the camp meals with her teenagers. Hardly delectable. Still, it had always been a life she enjoyed—*her* life. Tonight it seemed so foreign, so unreal.

After coffee and fresh raspberries and a sinful, buttery hazelnut torte were served, Reuben Kirk rose to address his guests. There were perhaps a dozen gathered at the table.

"Thank you all for coming," he said. Although he spoke in a smooth voice, there was an awkwardness about his manner that Sage found discomforting. He went on, "It's always a pleasure to see you. As some of you know, this is my first dinner since returning to California early last month. Thank you for making it so congenial, so . . . delightfully memorable."

There were polite murmurs across the table, and Sage wondered if she was the only one to hear the suppressed pain and fury in that soft, cultured voice. But glancing up at Jackson, she could see that he heard it, too. She felt her palms begin to sweat. Maybe she should have told Grandpa about tonight.

"Tonight is a special night for me for another reason," Reuben Kirk said with a smile that struck Sage as strained, if not utterly false. "More than a year ago I came into possession of the Blue Hill Series by Bradford Killibrew, which I assure you is as fine as has been rumored for years. In my opinion, the paintings are his most remarkable works to date."

Sage noticed how carefully he had phrased his words. "Came into possession of" could mean almost anything. Obviously more knowledgeable about art in general and

Bradford Killibrew in particular than she was, the guests could barely contain their excitement.

"I had never anticipated selling the series," he continued, with what Sage thought was another interesting choice of word. "However, I now find that, for personal reasons, I must. Therefore, tonight I would like to announce to you, some of my closest and dearest friends, that I will be holding a private showing of these works here next Sunday afternoon. You will be the first to see the series, and perhaps we'll have the opportunity to discuss a private sale. Please, all of you, come."

There wasn't a doubt in Sage's mind that not a single one of the guests at the dinner would miss the showing next Sunday. The damned vultures! She started to her feet, to yell at all of them for trying to cash in on her wronged grandfather's works, to demand that Reuben Kirk settle his feud with Bradford Killibrew before putting the paintings up for sale. It was unconscionable to sell an artist's work out from under him, but no less disgusting to *buy* a work whose ownership was being contested by the artist himself. They were all guilty, Sage thought angrily. But Jackson's hand shot out and grabbed her knee, holding her down as she fumed. She wondered if she'd turned red in the face, like Grandpa.

"It won't do any good," he whispered.

"I don't care," she muttered furiously. "They're all sharks."

"You sound like your grandfather. Look, my father isn't going to listen to reason."

She shot Jackson a look. "Who said anything about reason?"

"Sage . . ."

"Oh, all right," she said with a sigh. "I suppose you know your father better than I do."

The guests dispersed to the terrace for sherry and brandy and talk of Bradford Killibrew, the brilliant painter, the latest darling of the art world. Sage had her doubts whether Grandpa had been working toward such recognition. Knowing him, he'd consider it just another cross to bear. She listened to the speculation about the Blue Hill Series, Bradford Killibrew's future works, what the reclusive artist was like himself. Somehow the recognition didn't seem to matter, not to her. It was enough that Grandpa had realized his dream. That he'd painted, and painted well. Perhaps that was why he had no money, no trappings of success—none of that stuff was important to him. It made her respect him more.

"You're his granddaughter."

It was Reuben Kirk. Sage and Jackson turned to him at the same time and saw a man in a quiet rage. Reuben, elegantly dressed, the picture of propriety, stood rigid, clutching a wineglass. Jackson started to speak, but Sage stopped him. This was her battle; she was a Killibrew and damned proud of it.

"I'm Sage Killibrew," she said.

The elder Kirk's expression changed from controlled rage to visible distaste, then into a fury that was almost palpable. He choked out, "So you're spying for your grandfather."

Jackson gave her a quick look that told her to lie, but she couldn't. "I'm just trying to help him. And you, Mr. Kirk. Selling the Blue Hill Series will only exacerbate the situation. There's no need—"

"I don't need advice from you, young lady," he spat, never raising his voice, but each word shook with tension. His gaze shot up to his son's face. "And you? Are you on that man's side, too?"

Jackson sighed. "Father, I told you, I'm not taking sides. I don't know enough of what's eating at you two to decide who's right or who's wrong—or if either of you is right. Look, you can stand and pull the cool, debonair man-of-the-world act, but I know you're a damned hothead, just like Bradford."

"Enough." He breathed deeply, as if he'd been suffocating. "I'll thank you both to leave."

"You don't have to." Jackson's voice was low and deadly, and when he slammed his sherry glass onto one of the limestone tables, it shattered into scores of tiny, sharp shards. He wasn't cut. Without acknowledging the damage he turned to Sage. His expression was as hard and unyielding as his father's, but when he spoke, his voice was curiously gentle. "Come on, let's go."

She thought it best, for once, to keep her mouth shut. Coming between father and son wasn't her style, although she would have cheerfully kicked that smug old man into his glistening swimming pool. She'd done worse on less provocation.

"Well," she said, exhaling when they got to the car, "I guess there's no love lost between Reuben Kirk and Bradford Killibrew."

Jackson looked at her, then suddenly laughed. "You do have a way of reducing things to their essential elements."

"Well, you warned me about what I was getting into. I can see what you mean now. They're not going to listen to reason, either one of them."

"Any suggestions as to where we go from here?"

She turned and looked out at the Pacific surf crashing onto the sand, pleased that he was asking her instead of just telling her what he thought. Maybe she was wrong.

Maybe their relationship was different; maybe there was hope. She grinned sideways at him. "Deceit."

He laughed. "Spoken like a true Killibrew."

"*Or* a Kirk."

"A good point, but let's not argue," he said, "at least not until morning."

Then he started the car.

AT THE HOTEL he followed Sage to her room, and she didn't make any silly or false protests. She wasn't ready to see him off, not yet. At the very least, she wanted to talk to him—not about the Blue Hill Series or her eccentric grandfather and his own embittered father, but about him. Jackson Kirk. The man she'd had such strong feelings about since the moment she'd seen him. She wanted to listen to him tell her about himself, about who he had been, about who he was and who he hoped to be.

So she served him a glass of iced bottled water, went into the bathroom and peeled off her stockings and then climbed onto her bed in her bare feet and not-too-expensive dress. She crossed her legs in a tailor squat and leaned against the headboard. Jackson had already taken off his jacket and shoes and was lying across the foot of the bed. There'd never been a sexier man, Sage decided; there couldn't have been.

She made a comment about the weather, and that got them started. They talked about beaches and birds and music and cooking, and they talked about the nuclear arms problem and the plight of the homeless and the upcoming World Series. They talked about their jobs as if they were adventures, not work. Jackson was into a lot of things, but filmmaking was his passion. She could see that in his eyes, hear it in his voice. Yet he wasn't drawn to Hollywood and the big, expensive commercial films.

Rather, he wanted to do more documentaries, maybe a docudrama that would have a wider appeal. But his work, not commercial success, was what interested him. His ideas intrigued Sage, and she told him about her avocation as a photographer. It was just something she did for its own sake, not to earn money. They went on from there, and Sage could tell he'd learned a great deal from his father, whom he spoke of with respect. None of the frustration that had been exhibited earlier was visible.

Then they were telling funny stories, and sad ones, and ones that made no sense and had no point but were just something to talk about. To listen to. To dream to.

For a while after that they didn't talk at all. They sat with the drapes open so they could watch the sunset, so close but not touching, and just looked at each other. Without self-consciousness Sage stared into his violet eyes, now not so much impenetrable as mysterious, alluring; his scar no longer seemed menacing, but interesting. He'd gotten it while mountain-climbing in New Zealand. Had he told her that tonight? Or had she somehow just known it?

"What are you afraid of?" he asked, his quiet words hardly disturbing the stillness. He got up and shut the drapes, and she didn't have to ask why.

"I don't know what you mean."

When he came back to the bed, he stretched out down the middle, while she sat huddled among the pillows. Then he stopped, coming no closer. Her legs seemed suddenly very naked, prickly with sensations. "I think you do," he said, not accusing. "Is it me? Are you afraid of me, Sage?"

"No." Her answer was immediate, and emphatic. She stretched out her legs alongside him, her knees almost touching his shoulders, her toes at his waist. "No, I'm not. I haven't been, can't be."

"Then what is it?" His head propped up on one hand, he reached out and drew a little circle around her big toe. "What is it I'll see when I go to kiss you?"

"Longing, I hope," she said lightly.

He smiled. "Lurking behind the desire."

She wasn't going to joke her way out of this. If she wanted, expected, honesty from him, she had to give it in return. No one had ever told her it would be easy. "I'm not the namby-pamby type. I'm not afraid of you. It's ... myself, I suppose. I'm impulsive."

"Do tell," he said, squeezing her toes with an almost brotherly affection.

"Not just about helping grandfathers in need, either. About men. I, well, I have this seemingly fatal attraction to rogues. Auntie Killibrew says it's the fate of Killibrew women, but she's talking about a romanticized rogue. You know, someone you'd meet in the movies, not Colorado. Jackson ... Jackson, you creep, are you laughing?"

He stopped long enough to answer. "Darling ... rogues? Auntie Killibrew?"

"Grandpa's sister. She taught school for years, and after she retired, she encouraged Summerfield, my uncle, to revitalize Summerfield Shoe and sort of was a moving force behind Juniper's romance with Calvin Gilliam—they were married last summer—and she's stingy and she has a drafty old house in Portsmouth and a drafty little cottage in Maine. I wouldn't call her likable so much as ... interesting."

"Is she one of the reasons Bradford bolted?"

Sage pursed her lips at him. "I never said we were an ordinary family."

"You didn't have to. Now go on. What's this about rogues?"

"Here I was baring my soul to you . . ."

"I'm sorry. Honestly. Tell me about your rogues."

She sighed. "You can be such an ass, Jackson Kirk."

The bed creaking, he crawled up over her out-stretched legs and settled across her lap. "Not a rogue?"

"Not the kind of rogue I generally meet up with. They're *real* rogues."

"And you usually fall for them."

"Fall might be a tad too strong. Let's just say by the time I realize what kind of individual I'm involved with, I'm already involved. Not *involved* involved, you understand, just involved enough that I kick myself and promise that it won't happen again. We're not talking about long-term relationships here."

"Just your attraction, based on your great-aunt's view of genetics, to rogues."

"Right."

"And I'm a rogue."

"But not a real rogue."

"One of Auntie's rogues."

"Mmm. At least I think so. You see, that's the point. I'm not sure I know the difference. I decide a person's character on impulse, and I've been wrong often enough to doubt myself, especially when it comes to men with impenetrable eyes and lean hips."

He sat up straight, legs still across her lap, but so that they were eye to eye. "If I were one of your real rogues, would I be sitting here talking to you about your fears? No, I'd be loving the daylights out of you—which is a far more delicate way of putting it than a 'real' rogue would."

"You have a point."

"If I were a 'real' rogue, I'd have pitched you to the tigers that morning at the zoo. I'd have followed through with my threat and hauled you up to my room when I caught you snooping in my study."

She grinned. "You'd have made love to me under the bougainvillea."

"Well, I can't say I would have or wouldn't have, since Father interrupted—"

"Jackson!"

He laughed, kissed her lightly on the mouth. "You do see my point?"

"I do. You're one of Auntie's rogues."

"Which means you're doomed, doesn't it?"

"I'd like to think of it as fated."

"Fated or doomed," he said, his voice dropping to a murmur as he moved in closer. "According to your Auntie Killibrew, you're going to fall as madly in love with me as I'm falling with you."

His mouth found hers, and she rolled with him down onto the bed, away from the pillows. No words were called for. It wouldn't have mattered if there had been; she couldn't speak. She could only feel the flow of emotions and sensations inundating her with a rush of welcome, wet warmth. Her lips parted against his, and her tongue went out, seeking, exploring. He responded with a moan and opened his mouth, letting her go in deeper, begging her to. She responded.

"I can't get enough of you," he said, breaking the kiss for only a few seconds.

She gently pulled his mouth back to hers and, as she resumed the kiss, stroked his hair with her fingers, then let them trail lightly, erotically, down his neck. His hands moved up and down her sides, from under her arms to just above her knees, drawing the hem of her dress gradually upward, until he was stroking the firm naked flesh of her thighs.

Raising himself slightly above her, their eyes locked, he slipped his fingers inside her underpants at her hips, and slowly pulled them down and off. The cool air and the heat of his gaze further excited her. Then he slid one hand between her legs, and two fingers found that hot, throbbing spot, at first just touching it, then circling, then rubbing gently, rapidly.

She cried out. "Don't stop . . . please don't stop."

He lowered just his open mouth to hers and flicked out his tongue, then pulled back, straddling her, so all that touched her was his tongue and his fingers, moving in the same erotic, primitive rhythm. She began to sway with it as waves of arousal crashed over her.

Then he pushed her dress up further so that her taut abdomen was bared to him, and he brought his mouth to it, flicking his tongue along the smooth skin, edging lower. She was bursting with anticipation. Her thighs were parted, all of her waiting impatiently, crying out for him.

And slowly he came to her, his tongue taking over where his fingers had been, using the same technique, the same rhythm. She went with the feelings inside her, the love and the passion, communicating them to him in the most primitive of ways. She could hear him moan softly in response, in union with her, as he brought her to the edge of the precipice.

He raised himself off her. And in seconds he'd pulled off his pants and briefs and returned to her. She knew what he wanted, what she wanted to give him.

"I want you to make love to me . . . I want to feel you inside me." She smiled and reached up to touch his cheek. "And I want to make love to you."

It was all he needed to hear, all she needed to say. Holding her, Jackson reached for his pants, groping for the pocket that contained several small foil packets. Sage helped him arrange protection, stroking erotically all the while. Then he knelt between her thighs, pressing against her moistness. She guided him into her. Together they plunged off the precipice, into light and freedom and ecstasy, floating, then spinning, then rocking, crying out, exploding... until at last they landed in a cool bed of softness and just lay still.

Sage moved first. Jackson was lying beside her, one arm flung over her chest, just beneath her breasts. It felt right there. *He* felt right. "Are you asleep?" she whispered.

He stirred. "No."

"It's getting chilly. I need to get under the blankets."

"Do you want me to leave?" He was sitting up now, fully alert.

She grinned, shaking her head. "Uh-uh. You can come under the covers with me."

He grinned back. "I imagine I can."

"You dirty dog, you," she said, realizing now her unintentional double-entendre.

"Shall we do this thing right next time?"

"I didn't think we did so bad."

"We did beautifully, magnificently," he said. He brushed his fingertips across her breasts. "But we're going to ruin two perfectly good outfits if we're not careful."

"Ahh."

"You don't have forty thousand dollars tucked inside that dress, do you?"

"Of course not."

He dropped his hand down to her thighs. "Then off with it, woman."

She laughed and peeled off her dress, and by the time she was finished, somehow he had taken his shirt off, too, and put several small foil packets on the bedside table. They made love again that night, not once more, but twice . . . and again sometime in the cool hours of dawn.

9

SAGE ORDERED a light breakfast, not because she wasn't hungry—she was famished—but because she thought it best to introduce food to her stomach gradually after last night. She had never felt so satiated, so alive . . . so ravenous. But she didn't want to upset the delicate balance in her system by stuffing herself. She'd eat her muffin, fresh fruit and coffee, and then see how she felt.

"Grandpa better not show up," she said.

Jackson smiled at her from across the table, his hair wild and dark. "Why not?"

"He'd know in a minute what we'd been up to."

He laughed. "I suspect you're right. Do you care?"

"He's highly combustible as it is," she said, adding cream to her coffee. Her hand trembled, just a little, and she was glad she was in good physical shape. Four bouts of lovemaking would knock the wind out of any woman. Jackson himself looked as if he could use a few hours in bed . . . alone. "I don't see any point in adding more fuel to his fire. He'd call me a traitor, you a scoundrel, and go off on his own to do God knows what. If there's any chance of settling this feud he and your father are having, it will require some discretion on our part."

"Agreed."

There was that half smile again, and even with all that had transpired between them, Sage could feel herself responding to it, wanting him. Just the smallest gesture could electrify her. It was incredible, and perhaps a little frightening.

"Do you have any plans for the day?" Jackson asked.

She was savoring a slice of melon. "Just a call to Colorado. I have a light schedule right now, but I need to cancel a couple of classes since it looks as if I'll be here at least through the week. This is one of those times a flexible schedule comes in handy. What about you?"

"I'm not sure what I'll do. I have plenty of work, of course, but it seems to me if we're going to find a peaceful solution to the Bradford Killibrew-Reuben Kirk quarrel, we'd better get started. Sunday isn't that far off, and if the press gets hold of this—"

"My God, I can just imagine," Sage said without relish. "If Grandpa gets more widely known to the public, it'll come out that he started Killibrew Traders and snuck off twenty years ago—that'll be quite enough for the family to handle. But a feud with an Academy Award-winning director—that's just downright embarrassing. I suppose we should come up with some kind of strategy for dealing with this mess, don't you?"

"Yes, but I could use some fresh ideas."

She drank some coffee and settled back in her chair, thinking. "I could get my brother-in-law out here to buy the Blue Hill Series. He can afford to pay market value and Grandpa's never met him, so he wouldn't necessarily have to know what's going on. And his name's Cal Gilliam, not Killibrew, so your father wouldn't be suspicious, either. I know Cal. He'd be glad to turn the series back over to Grandpa."

"I hate to say it, Sage, but it won't work." Jackson had devoured most of his breakfast and was working on his second cup of coffee. He seemed so physical, so exciting, so *alive*. "First of all, Bradford wants more than just to get the series back—he wants revenge. Having your brother-in-law buy the paintings at their market value won't give your grandfather any satisfaction. Second, the showing on Sunday is a private one. I've heard of Cal Gilliam, and I'm sure he has connections, but my father would be sure to find out who he is. He's already suspicious of virtually everyone around him."

"Damn. But I see your point."

"It's a sticky problem, I know."

"What about you—any ideas?"

A distant, closed look came into those violet eyes, brighter than ever this morning, and Sage could feel him drifting away from her, not far, but still it hurt. Something had occurred to him—a passing thought, an idea, a strategy—that he wasn't willing to share with her.

"Frankly," he said, "I think the best course of action is for you to find out from your grandfather what's really going on between him and my father. There has to be a *reason* my father won't sell him back the paintings as agreed."

"Maybe he's just ornery. Maybe he wants to make a profit."

"No, I can't believe that. You've seen for yourself my father doesn't need the money. It's almost as if *he's* out for revenge, too, but I honestly can't fathom what Bradford could have done to offend him this badly. They've been friends for too many years, you know. Even before I met Bradford, they were friends. Granted, it's been a damned volatile friendship, but still, orneriness and profit aren't sufficient motives for this kind of mutual hatred." Jackson threw up his hands, anger and frustration showing now in his face. "I tried to talk to Father about it, but he won't budge—just asks me to kindly butt out."

"All right, I can try to get Grandpa to talk, but I doubt it'll be easy."

He smiled. "It definitely won't be easy, but it's worth a try."

"And what will you do?"

"I'll see what I can do to keep the paintings off the market until this thing can be resolved, one way or the other."

He was hedging, the distant look back. And, without words, was asking her not to press him. But Sage had never been one to take a hint, subtle or flagrant. She leaned forward, folding her hands in front of her plate. "Like what?"

"I don't think I'd better say."

The words were kindly delivered, even regretfully, but still they stung. She sat back. "Because you don't trust me."

"That's not it."

"You think if you tell me, I'll tell Grandpa."

"Sage, for heaven's sake, it's pretty obvious your loyalties lie with him. I have no quarrel with that; it's perfectly understandable."

"And you think you're objective."

"Neutral."

"Humbug," she said, annoyed. "If you have a plan and you don't want me to tell my grandfather, I won't."

"Look, at this stage, I wouldn't even call it a plan. It's probably just another wild-goose chase—nothing I've thought out too clearly. Give me some space, okay?"

Sage was nothing if not relentless. "You're afraid of looking impulsive. Jackson, this is *me* you're talking to! The one who came to San Diego with a briefcase full of Monopoly money!"

"Just let me do what I have to do, Sage," he said quietly, equally immovable. "Trust *me*."

"Fine," she said angrily, snatching up her handbag. "You do what you have to do. I'll do what *I* have to do. Obviously last night was just a damned good roll in the hay for you and didn't mean a thing."

She was on her feet and slamming past him, but he caught her by the wrist and spun her around to face him. Her breath was coming in gasps. She was furious and hurt. If she'd taken his hint and not pressed him, he wouldn't have had to come right out and tell her he wasn't talking. She supposed she should appreciate his honesty, if not his frankness: he hadn't thought up a lie that would have pacified her, which had been his previous strategy. But she was too tired and too irritated and too hurt to appreciate such subtleties. Damn the man, she thought. Maybe she was wrong; maybe he wasn't one of Auntie's rogues but a real one. A cad like the others she'd booted none too gently out of her life. After all that had gone on between them—the loving and sharing and *everything*—why in blazes couldn't he talk?

"Sage," he said, looking up at her with an expression of such calm and reason she could have kicked him. But the look in his eyes stopped her. There was anguish there. He went on softly, "Last night meant everything to me."

"I'd like to believe you, Jackson, but how can I when you won't believe me?"

And she stalked off, leaving him with the bill. Petty revenge ran in the family, she thought—hers and his.

THE NEW MARINA Grandpa Killibrew had chosen wasn't one of La Jolla's best, but even so, Sage had no trouble picking out his boat. Not only did she somehow anticipate its sea-weathered look, but it was called, in a decidedly unexpected touch of sentimentality, Traders. Juniper would be pleased.

Grandpa was sitting out on his deck, where the paint was badly peeling, looking out at the other classier boats in the marina, or just enjoying the perfect weather, when Sage joined him. "Good morning," she said.

He squinted up at her. "Good morning, thunder-cloud."

The perspicacity of an artist, she thought; he'd sensed her foul mood in an instant. His bluntness cheered her. "It's already been a rough morning."

"So I see. Want anything?"

It hadn't taken long for her to regret running out on her breakfast, if not Jackson Kirk. She should have finished eating, and probably should have followed Jackson. "You wouldn't by any chance have anything to eat?"

"A veritable feast." He disappeared below.

Sage found a weather-beaten deck chair, its green fabric seat and back bleached almost colorless by the sun, and unfolded it. Half-expecting to end up on the floor, she was surprised to find it held her weight. She let the ocean smells and the soft breeze soothe her taut nerves. She hadn't forgiven Jackson for being so closemouthed, but she'd quit thinking it signaled that last night had no meaning for him. That was pure paranoia on her part. It was true she was still annoyed with him, but she'd also accepted that their relationship was going to be hard to sort out with her grandfather and his father at each other's throat. And even without that mess they'd have had their problems.

Grandpa reappeared, whistling, with two paper plates and two paper cups. He handed Sage hers: turkey, lettuce and tomato on thick slabs of whole grain bread slathered with mustard, and something that appeared to be cold cucumber soup.

"I've got to go back down for the tea," he said.

"Grandpa, it's ten o'clock."

"So?"

"I was thinking more of, well, breakfast."

"I've been up since four."

"I haven't."

"You're on my boat, aren't you?"

"All right, all right. Go fetch the tea. Um, what kind is it?"

"Iced." He ducked below.

He returned with two tall plastic glasses filled with, thank heavens, ordinary iced tea. "Do all up-and-coming painters live like this?" she asked.

"If they're smart," Grandpa replied promptly, taking a seat. "And who says I'm only 'up and coming'?"

She laughed. "You always did have a high opinion of yourself. Did you sail this bucket all the way from South America?"

"That I did. It took awhile, but I made it. I love the sea."

"I remember," she said, trying her sandwich. It was hearty enough; maybe just what she needed after all. "I'm surprised Reuben Kirk didn't hire a pirate ship to blow you out of the water."

Her grandfather looked at her, his thick white eyebrows furrowed so that they came together in a straight line, not condemning, but curious. "So you've met the villain, have you?"

Sage knew she had to be careful, but she wanted to be honest, too. Despite her ties to Jackson—just because she'd stalked out on him didn't mean she was finished with him!—she hadn't forsaken her grandfather and his quest for his paintings. But she did want more information. The only problem was how to get it. She swallowed and said, "Just briefly. We—"

Grandpa's eyebrows tilted into a V as his frown deepened. "He followed you, you know."

Suddenly Sage realized he was looking not at her but at something behind her. "Reuben Kirk? But that's impossible—"

"No, the young one."

"*Jackson!*" She swung around, her chair creaking dangerously, but Jackson wasn't on the pier, and if his Alfa Romeo had been in the marina lot, it was gone now.

"Knows where I am now," Grandpa muttered.

Sage turned back to him. "It's my fault, I'm sorry." She tried to conceal her disappointment and anger with Jackson. How could he be so devious? Never mind that only a moment before she'd been regretting she hadn't followed him. *He* had followed her! "He had no right."

"Course he didn't, but he's a Kirk."

She set her plate down on a bench that ran around the perimeter of the deck and concentrated on her iced tea, her appetite suddenly gone. "Grandpa, I can't go on like this. I'm on your side, you know that, but if you want my help, you're going to have to give me some facts. I want the whole story."

He grunted. "You going to tell Kirk?"

"Which one?"

"Yours."

"You're determined to be irritating this morning, aren't you? As far as I'm concerned, they're both *your* Kirks. But I know who you mean. Jackson would like to know your story—and I think he has a right to." She put aside her own confused feelings and tried to be objective. "He seems to be trying to maintain some sort of neutrality. I don't think he wants you or his father to do anything that could land you both in serious trouble. However, if you ask me not to tell him, I won't—especially if he's going to do things like following me."

To her relief Grandpa didn't ask her how Jackson Kirk had been able to follow her. Instead, in a sudden, impatient move, he heaved the rest of his iced tea over the side of the boat into the Pacific. "I don't care what you do," he said, watching the ice sink. "Tell him. It won't matter. He might as well know what a contemptible thing his father's done."

Sage resisted the urge to try to maneuver him into giving her the bare facts more quickly; she'd had about enough of his spouting off. But Grandpa wasn't one to be rushed. Like most Killibrews, he did things only in his own sweet time. Judiciously she said nothing.

"Ana Luiza Dantas." Grandpa sighed at the cloudless blue sky. "That's what all this is about."

"A woman?"

"Reuben's second wife. She had no business being in the same room with that man, much less marrying him. I introduced them, you know. One of my more regrettable actions. Ana has one of those sensitive, incisive minds that's so rare today. But she's also young and very pretty. Reuben was still smarting after his first wife, Frances, had walked out on him. Now *there's* a woman who could handle the old crank, but she'd had her fill, I suppose, after thirty-seven years and packed up and left for San Francisco."

"Jackson's mother."

"Yes, he's their only child."

"I don't even know how old he is," she mused.

"Thirty-four. The eyes are from his mother."

Sage blushed, wondering how he'd known that was exactly what she'd been thinking. Having Grandpa back among the Killibrews might not be such a good thing after all. If they thought Auntie was an astute observer . . .

"Anyway," Grandpa went on, stretching out his bony legs, "they had one of those whirlwind courtships and got married much too soon. I knew it was wrong from the start, but I didn't interfere, of course."

Sage tried not to smile. Despite his long absence from his family, Grandpa had been the original of what he called the "meddlesome" Killibrews. "I can't imagine that you would have."

Grandpa chose to ignore the affectionate note of sarcasm in her words. "We'd been friends for a while, Ana and I, and after her marriage I encouraged her to do things on her own, not to let herself get lost in Reuben's fame and reputation. She needed her own sense of self. She's young, not a hard case like Frances. Anyway, Ana was interested in helping unwed mothers in São Paulo and got involved with a privately run home—a place that offered the young women a clean place to live, hope for the future, dignity. Reuben didn't mind at first, but when Ana needed money to keep the home from going under, she came to me. I knew then something was wrong."

"Had to be if she came to you," Sage interjected. "Reuben Kirk has more money than you do."

"Infinitely, and he's good with money. Me—easy come, easy go."

"It wasn't always like that."

"No, but I learned there's more to life than a fat bank account, which is something you've always seemed to know." He smiled at her, then quickly shoved aside any sentimentality, any grandfatherly feelings. "Reuben thought Ana was spending too much time at the home and not enough time with him, getting too involved. It was just plain jealousy and insecurity. He hasn't been himself since Frances's defection. But Ana's never saved a penny of her own, and when Reuben wouldn't help her—"

"She came to you, and you did."

He shrugged. "Sure. The home was desperate—they'd have closed without an infusion of funds."

For a moment she heard a hint of the old Bradford Killibrew, the sharp-minded Yankee businessman applying those keen instincts to a charitable organization, to people in need. Sage's heart warmed toward him. He'd left his family for twenty years, but he was a good man, a better man, perhaps, than he might have been if he'd stayed. "The home needed forty thousand just to stay alive, which I didn't have at the time. So I took the Blue Hill Series to Reuben. We were friends, you understand, and I thought I could trust him to make a deal. I told him I needed some cash, and without even asking for what, he agreed to pay forty thousand for the series, with the understanding that when I pulled the money together, he'd sell them back to me for the same price."

"He can sell *each* of them for three times that price—"

"I know that."

"Didn't Reuben ask you what the money was for?"

Grandpa squirmed a little, shaking his head.

"And when he found out, he felt betrayed." Sage sighed. "I can't say I blame him. I mean, he's gone a little far in his revenge, but still, in his position I'd have felt used. In his mind, you were helping his wife go against him, and if he was feeling insecure, anyway, well, he must have been furious when he found out."

"It's worse than that," Grandpa said quietly. "Right after she got the money and gave it to the home, Ana realized there was hope the home could survive and that that was where she belonged, not with Reuben. She left him—permanently. She's working at the home now, living there, doing what she feels she has to. She and Reuben had been drifting apart from the beginning. She had to find an identity and commitments of her own, but Reuben didn't see it that way. When he found out where she'd gotten the funds, he blamed me for encouraging her."

"Wasn't he angry with her, too?"

"No, to him Ana was more like a child, someone he could count on to need him. Frances had always been very independent, and he thought maybe someone exactly the opposite wouldn't leave him as she had. But Ana proved that she could get along on her own, too. He didn't see that she was not only capable of making her own decisions about her life, but had to. Otherwise, she'd have suffocated. Reuben didn't have her best interests at heart, just his own. He was too wrapped up in his own suffering to see anyone else's needs. It was less damaging to his ego to blame me than to accept her as a functioning adult." He grinned suddenly. "Don't look so surprised, Sage. I may grunt and fume a lot, but I do have a brain in my head."

She smiled. "You're not just a mad eccentric. So when he found out what had happened, Reuben reneged on his end of the deal you'd made."

"Snuck off to California. I found out where he'd slithered off to, though, and followed him out here."

"To get your paintings."

"Damn right."

"I can understand your anger—but I can understand Reuben's, too. It can't have been easy to watch a second marriage dissolve so quickly after the first, and it must have been only natural to want to find anyone to blame but himself."

"It wasn't his fault," Grandpa interjected. "It wasn't anyone's fault—not his, not Ana's, not mine. Reuben was on the rebound from Frances and he and Ana married on impulse. There's no right and wrong in the situation, just what was—something the old coot refuses to see."

"Maybe he will, in time."

Grandpa's eyebrows went up, and his face reddened in a sudden rush of frustration. *"I don't have time!"*

Sage sighed, wriggling on the rickety chair. "Less than you might even think, Grandpa. Reuben's having a private showing of the Blue Hill Series next Sunday. He means to sell it."

"The wretch!" Grandpa clenched his fists, barely able to speak. "Tell me everything."

As Sage related the events of the previous evening— or at least some of the events—her grandfather quickly forgot his openness and understanding of a moment ago and turned increasingly deeper shades of purple. What transpired between her and Jackson was conveniently edited out of her rendition. It was, she concluded, immaterial.

"I'm sorry, Grandpa," she said when she'd finished. "I just don't know what to do next."

"Do?" He scrambled to his feet, as nimble as a man one-third his age, and rubbed his stubbly jaw in thought. "There's only one thing to do, of course: get to this showing somehow and restore my paintings to their rightful owner."

"Steal them, you mean. Grandpa, Kirk could have you arrested. You could go to jail."

"Bah."

"You could, and you know it. He's obviously incredibly embittered and hurt. If you just give him some time—"

"I've given him more than six months!"

"To recover from not one but *two* broken marriages? That's not enough time. Look, Jackson and I both want to help resolve this situation peacefully. Let us try."

"You've decided to trust him, have you?"

"More or less. At least give us a chance."

Grandpa sighed, pacing, then stopped abruptly and pivoted to face his granddaughter. "Okay, I will. You have until Sunday afternoon." He wagged a long finger at her. "But mark my words, Sage. I intend to get those paintings back, one way or another. I've been patient damned long enough."

"You've *waited* long enough, but I doubt you've ever been patient," she muttered. "Grandpa, why all the fuss about the Blue Hill Series? You said yourself it isn't the money, and if you understand Reuben Kirk's pain, why not just let it go and paint another series?"

"This one's special to me, that's why. And I mean to get it back."

It was all he would say. He made her sit down and map out Reuben Kirk's house and grounds, and together they made preliminary plans for breaking into the place. All Sage could think of was that Jackson would explode if he found out. And Reuben Kirk—God only knew what he'd do. Call the police, shoot them both as trespassers. But she had never seen her grandfather quite as delighted as when he was plotting how to "thwart," as he called it, his one-time closest friend. He was occupied, at least.

And she—and Jackson, if he was willing—had four more days to find a solution.

When she returned to the Hotel Del, there was a message waiting from him. "Here's the key to my house. I'm going to be out of town for a couple of days. Why don't you stay there until I get back? When I do, I'll tell you everything. Promise. See you soon. Jackson."

Out of town for a couple of days! Where? Why? Sage crumpled up the note and wished she could stomp on it, but there were too many people around. *What* was Jackson up to now? And why hadn't he told her?

She growled in frustration and marched up to her room, where she packed her things. Then she checked out and drove over to Jackson's house, where the sun was dazzling and the flowers blooming and the price just right. She swung in the hammock and thought up plots against him. If he wasn't going to cooperate with her, then she didn't feel any obligation to cooperate with him.

By Sunday, she thought, she and Grandpa Killibrew would have a plan intact to obtain justice—or, in other words, to get the Blue Hill Series back. Jackson could do as he pleased.

That decided, she fell asleep. To her distress she dreamed not about stolen paintings and long lost grandfathers, but about irresistible scoundrels with violet eyes.

10

SAGE WAS LYING in the rope hammock just beyond the terrace in Jackson's backyard, eating a chocolate bar and reading a paperback bestseller, when she heard the back door creak. Lifting her eyes from a juicy scene, she peered over her book as Jackson moved toward her. She inhaled sharply, noticing everything about him. The flash of his eyes, his tousled hair, his smooth walk, his sheer physical presence.

"Don't you look the picture of innocence," he said, as though he couldn't believe what he was seeing, which was just as well. An hour earlier he'd have caught her returning from her latest plotting session on the decrepit *Traders*. As Grandpa said, with two Killibrews on the case, the Kirks were doomed.

She bit off a chunk of candy bar. "I'm pretending I'm on vacation."

Jackson came closer, his expression unreadable, but she sensed a level of seriousness, even nervousness. "I wondered if you'd be here."

"The only other choices were staying at the Hotel Del, which does not accept Monopoly money for payment; heading back to Colorado, which would be akin to retreating and Killibrews, as you've no doubt surmised, never retreat; or staying with Grandpa, who would drive me crazy." She took another bite of candy bar and squinted up at him. He was everything she remembered, had dreamed about . . . everything. "So here I am."

Jackson gave her a half smile. "Indeed."

"You don't look very rested for a man who's been away from me for two days."

That remark broadened the smile. "I could take that several ways."

"You could."

"Do you want to know where I've been?"

"Of course, but I refuse to ask. You'd either clam up or lie—unless you want me to know, in which case you'll tell me, anyway."

"How well you know me after such a short time. But I suppose it's an indication of how alike we are." He plucked the book from her fingers, any hint of nervousness gone. "Come on, I'd like you to meet my mother."

Sage almost fell out of the hammock, but Jackson caught her by the waist, steadying her—at least in a certain sense. She didn't fall over. But in another sense his brief touch rocked her to her very core, and she felt decidedly unsteady. Maybe they'd had a setback in the trust department, but all was well in the sexual excitement department. She wanted him as much as ever. More.

"Well," she said with a choked lightness. "Welcome home."

He flicked a kiss on her cheek near a stray lock of hair. "Glad to be back."

In the kitchen a woman Jackson introduced as Frances Kirk, his mother, was preparing a coffee tray. She was dark and tall, although not as tall as Sage, and had refined manners and speech. Her eyes were violet, a shade lighter than her son's, not as thickly lashed, not as roguish. And she was pleasant.

"Let's go into the library," she said. "As I told Jackson, I doubt I can have a positive influence on this situation. Reuben can barely stand to be around me, and Bradford, well, I'm sure you know your grandfather, Sage. He listens to no one."

Jackson took the tray. "If Bradford Killibrew will listen to anyone, it'll be you, Mother. As for Father, you know as well as I do he's always listened to you. He respects your judgment."

Frances smiled wryly. "My judgment doesn't usually involve telling him he's acting like a perfect ass."

They settled in the library, Frances on a worn leather chair, Sage on the floor. Jackson sat on the floor with his back against the couch, his shoulder rubbing against Sage's knee. She tried not to let his touch distract her. She thought Frances had a point about her ex-husband but decided it would be more polite not to say so.

"You're our last hope, Mother," Jackson said.

Not according to Grandpa, Sage thought. He figured that he was his own last hope and that Plan D—the one he'd cooked up with her—was a winner. Mostly it involved getting to his paintings on Sunday before Reuben could take bids on them, which was a whole lot tougher than it sounded. He didn't need Frances Kirk or anyone trying to talk him out of his plan, either, but Sage had no intention of interfering. With Jackson back she was willing to throw herself into trying to resolve the differences between the elder Kirk and Killibrew before the showing—and before they could put Plan D into effect. But she had also gotten to know her grandfather better during the past two days. He was going to get his paintings back, and he was going to do it his way.

"I'll do what I can, I told you that." Frances wore a chic but not flashy designer suit, obviously a woman of taste and dignity. "But no promises—and don't expect any miracles."

"You don't have to worry about that," Jackson muttered.

His mother smiled. "What about you, Sage? Do you have any ideas?"

Sage shrugged, leaning forward to pour herself coffee. "Pistols at fifty paces?"

"Don't think I haven't thought of it," Frances put in. "For as long as those two have been friends, they've fought about everything from the Third World debt to how fast the grass grows. They'd argue with a post if there wasn't anyone else around."

Sage herself had caught Grandpa grumbling at a frayed length of rope that wouldn't cooperate with him and loosen up from the knot he'd tied it into. The poor thing was so damned old and limp it couldn't. Sage had quietly suggested purchasing a new rope, but he'd looked at her as if she were mad. Then what would he have to fuss at?

"They're both too much alike. Well," Frances said heavily, rising, "I'll do what I can."

Jackson rose. "When do you plan to start? We only have until Sunday."

"Tonight, I suppose."

"Father?"

"Good heavens, no. I'll deal with him in the morning." Again she offered that wry, attractive smile. She was an intelligent and sensitive woman—a psychologist, Grandpa had said. Apparently she'd left Reuben to pursue her doctorate; he hadn't wanted to leave Brazil. Neither had been able to compromise, and the next thing Grandpa knew, they were filing for divorce. She went on, "I wouldn't want to make him feel awkward by showing up in the evening, you know. No, I'll go on over to Bradford's boat."

"You'll spend the night here, of course."

Her eyes flickered at Sage, then back to her son. "No, I'll just borrow a mat from Bradford. He has such a knack for reducing life to its essential elements. It'll be a nice change."

"Mother, are you sure?"

"Jackson, somehow I've managed to last all these years and even raise you without your advice and worry. I'll be fine. I could use a car, though."

He handed her the keys to his Alfa Romeo and saw her off, and Sage stayed put lest either of them think to ask what she'd been up to for the past two days. Or what she knew about the Kirk-Killibrew feud. Or anything. She wasn't up to answering questions. She was too preoccupied with the back view of Jackson's tall, lean frame.

Sage heard the Alfa Romeo back out of the driveway, and in another moment Jackson returned to the library. She was still rooted to her spot. Looking up at him in the doorway, she asked, "Hungry?"

"Not for food."

She laughed. "Ah-ha. Well, I know what you mean."

"Do you?" He squatted in front of her, catcher-style, and his expression was serious as he took her hands by the fingertips. "I'm sorry, Sage, for how I lit out of here on Tuesday. I just—This whole thing has me crazy. My father, your grandfather. You."

"Me!"

He smiled. "Yes, you."

And leaning forward, he kissed her lightly on the mouth. "Definitely you," he said.

She kissed him back, carefully. "You're going to tip over and smoosh me."

"Now there's an idea."

He kissed her again, leaning too far forward, and whether by accident or on purpose she couldn't say, he couldn't right himself. She had to catch him by the waist and take him with her as his weight sent her backward, flat out on the floor. The rug was thick and soft, and his weight on her felt good.

She grinned at him, his face close to hers, his body touching the whole length of hers. "I trust you don't have a wrestling match in mind," she said. "You've already got me pretty well pinned."

"Good."

His mouth found hers again, and that was all she felt. Mouth and lips and tongue, hot and probing, and then in seconds, she was naked on the carpet. In another few seconds he was naked, too, hard and ready. He gently moved over her, then plunged into her with a firm thrust and they both cried out with joy and ecstasy. They moved in unison, responding wildly to every touch, every moan, until they suddenly exploded together, filling the air with their shuddering cries, and then the silence of their satiation, punctuated only by their deep gasps for air.

Then they gathered their clothes and, laughing, went upstairs to make love again on the big platform bed in Jackson's room. Afterward they decided they'd better go out to dinner. If they didn't, they might never eat again.

"YOU DON'T THINK there's anything going on between your mother and my grandfather, do you?" Sage asked.

They were in a small, quiet restaurant in the center of Coronado, and both had ordered fresh fish and white wine, a much needed light meal after their lovemaking. Jackson grimaced at her suggestion. "Isn't this mess complicated enough without *that*?"

"Well, she is spending the night on his boat."

"They're friends."

"Yes, but you've seen his boat. I mean, would *you* spend the night on it without a damned good reason?"

"I should think saving an ex-husband and an old friend from jail—or worse—would be reason enough."

Sage grinned. "My, my, aren't we touchy when the subject of our mama's love life comes up."

He frowned at her. "Don't be an ass."

"Sorry." She meant it. "Do you really think she has a chance at making peace between those two?"

"A remote one, but better than any we've got," he said without enthusiasm. "I don't know, I'm about ready to wash my hands of the entire business and spirit you off to the South Seas."

"To visit your friend who collects ants."

"He studies them."

"Whatever."

"Actually, I was thinking more in terms of making love on isolated beaches."

Her heart skipped a beat. Did he see their relationship in that light? Did she? All she knew was that going back to Colorado and picking up where she'd left off was no longer a high-priority option. "What would we do for money?"

"Work here and there. Imagine the team we'd make: Sage Killibrew, mountain woman, and Jackson Kirk, rogue."

She laughed. "I've decided I like scoundrel better."

He laughed, too, softly, as his gaze reached her from across the linen-covered table. "You're outrageous, you know that, don't you? I suppose I'll have to introduce you to some *real* scoundrels."

"You'd better watch out. I might run off with them. It's my worst weakness. My parents are in the South Seas, you know."

"Doing what?"

"My mother's a doctor." Then she told him about their call to bring medicine to people who would otherwise go without. "I visited them once, in the Philippines. They come home on occasion, but I doubt they'll ever stay. They love what they're doing. I used to think about becoming a doctor and joining them, but, I don't know, I never seemed to get around to it. I'm not real disciplined about studying stuff. Too impatient, I guess."

He smiled gently with understanding. "Do you see yourself spending the rest of your life in the mountains?"

"I don't know. Maybe. Not doing what I'm doing now, not forever, anyway. I think I might lose patience and start pitching kids off mountaintops." She grinned irreverently as his eyes widened. "Just kidding, Kirk. I do enough different kinds of things with enough different kinds of people that I don't get bored or burned out. Sometimes I think about starting up my own camp, something that would combine different disciplines, but I wouldn't want to confine it to the Rockies. Who knows? Maybe I'll take a bunch of kids to the South Seas to study nature and paint sunsets."

"But you don't see yourself in a nine-to-five job?"

"Uh-uh. Juniper would hire me in a flash—not because I'm any good, but because I'm family. Wouldn't work. No, about the only other thing I imagine is doing more with my photography, but I don't know. It's such a great avocation I'd hate to ruin it." She drank some wine, watching Jackson, glad they could talk like this.

"How 'bout you? I haven't exactly seen you punching a clock."

"Not my style," he said languidly.

"Ah-ha! Something we have in common!"

He stared into his glass, swirling the wine but not drinking. "Actually, I think we have a lot in common. Perhaps too much."

She groaned. "You've got to be kidding."

"No," he said, looking up at her, suddenly serious, "I'm not. We're both hard-headed and impulsive, both determined to get our own way, both always looking around the corner for the next adventure. There's no stability with us, Sage, no center."

"Are you saying I'd be happier with an investment banker?"

He laughed, but the melancholy was still in his eyes, and shook his head. "No, but how long before we're like my father and your grandfather, at one another's throats? I've been enjoying you, Sage, God knows. There's never been anyone like you in my life; there never will be. But I don't want to destroy you."

"Jackson, I'm intrepid," she replied, serious now herself. "Yes, I'm impulsive—and probably all those other things you say, too. But I relish every second we're together, even when you irritate the hell out of me. Maybe I've been enjoying the moment without considering the future . . . but isn't it a little early yet? Let's get to know each other first. Let's . . . I don't know, let's concentrate on making peace between the older generation of our families first."

He sighed. "You're right, but dammit, lady, it's getting so I can't imagine life without you."

"Good." She grinned. "And how very *un*-scoundrel-like of you."

After dinner they drove back to his house and walked along the beach, where the wind and the sea and the sand dispelled any lingering seriousness. They held hands and swung their arms, like teenagers. And Sage had to admit—wanted to—that she couldn't imagine life without Jackson, either.

"Are you going to tell me what you and your grandfather are plotting?" he asked.

She looked at him with mock innocence. "What makes you think we're plotting anything?"

"Genes."

"Let's just say I'm humoring him."

A sharp breeze tousled their hair, and they both looked wild and carefree. "Which means you're not going to tell me what he's up to."

"He asked me not to."

"If I'd confided I was going after my mother to talk her into intervening, would you have told him?"

"Of course not."

"Liar."

"Well, he might have dragged it out of me—accidentally on my part, of course. He's very sneaky."

Jackson made a little noise of agreement. "You know what he'd have done, don't you?"

She shook her head, watching the stars twinkling above the Pacific as she felt Jackson's firm, warm hand in hers. It seemed as if she belonged nowhere else but here, on this beach, with him. "I never try to predict Grandpa's actions," she said.

"I can't blame you for that, but I *know* he'd never have agreed to wait till Sunday to make his move if he knew Mother was on her way."

"Why, you sneaky scoundrel!" She kicked sand over his feet and swung in front of him, the wind blowing her hair all around her face. "You're trying to manipulate me into telling you Grandpa's plans! I haven't said a *word* about Sunday."

"So I'm right," he said, deadpan. "He is planning to make his move Sunday. It makes sense. Right now he doesn't know exactly where the paintings are, but since you've told him about the showing on Sunday, he knows damn well they'll be at the house then. Did he get you to draw a map of my father's house and grounds?"

Her hands flew to her hips in indignation. "I'm not telling you a thing!"

"You know," he went on mildly, the devil in his eyes, "I could tell Father and he could have the showing moved to another location—and I could suggest he make *me* promise not to tell *you*."

"You wouldn't dare."

"Oh, wouldn't I?"

"You don't trust me!"

"And you trust me?"

"Jackson, I promised my grandfather!"

"And I'm just suggesting what it would be like if the shoe was on the other foot! Wouldn't you do whatever you could to get me to tell you the location of the showing?"

"Well, yes, of course," she admitted, trying to tuck a stray lock behind her ear, but it was a hopeless cause. "But that's different."

"Why, because your grandfather's in the right and my father's in the wrong?"

"No, because ... Oh, hell, how am I supposed to know?" She threw up her arms in exasperation and let them flop down to her sides. "I've got a candle lit at both ends and *I'm* the one who's going to end up burned!"

"Sage ..."

"I hope your mother can work a miracle. I've been trying all week with Grandpa, but he's as stubborn as ever. He did give me a few more details—about Ana Luiza and her home for unwed mothers."

Jackson nodded. "My mother told me. Father blames Bradford for Ana's decision to leave. He thinks they might even have been having an affair."

"They weren't, although I don't suppose it matters. How did your mother know?"

"She didn't say. Friends, I would think. After thirty-seven years of marriage she and my father have a lot of mutual friends."

"One would think so." She sighed. "Anyway, you're right: Grandpa agreed not to act until the showing on Sunday."

Jackson's mouth settled into a straight, grim line. "And you believe him?"

"What choice do I have? I'm just hoping we can solve this thing by then so I—Well, never mind."

"So you don't have to play cat burglar?"

She spun around in the sand and marched off, not answering.

"That's all I need to do," he yelled at her retreating figure, "post bail for *both* of you!"

"You're presuming we'll get caught!" she yelled back.

"Damned right you'll get caught. Father's hired private security people. He *knows* Bradford will try something. Sage! Dammit, will you stop a minute and listen?"

She kept right on walking. She hadn't the faintest notion where she was headed, but she didn't care. At the moment she'd have rather walked to the edge of hell than do Jackson Kirk's bidding!

He actually growled in frustration: she wasn't the docile and easygoing type, and certainly not intimidated by him. "If you don't turn around and come back *now . . .*"

"You'll what?"

There was something distinctly cocky in her tone. She loved it. She'd show him, she would. She kept marching briskly along in the sand.

"I'll come after you is what!"

There was something profoundly self-assured in his tone. She ignored it.

And that was her first mistake. Her second was walking too close to the water. She heard his footsteps pounding in the sand behind her, but she thought she had a moment to sprint away—her third mistake. He caught her by her belt, heaved her up and pitched her into the water, which was icy cold. As she shivered, drenched to the waist, a wave came roaring toward her, but she scuttled away and ran up onto the sand.

She promised herself he, however, would get wet from head to toe, and went after him. He was laughing so hard, enjoying his victory, that he didn't notice how close she was or guess her intention until it was too late. Anchoring herself well, using all her strength and the element of surprise, she tripped him and sent him head over heels into a wave.

He came out dripping, his scoundrel's grin white and gleaming. "Woman," he said huskily, scooping her up into his arms, "I'm going to haul your beautiful butt up to my bed and make love to you until you can't stand up."

"My, my."

"What do you say to that?"

"I say let's get going before we freeze to death."

11

SAGE AWAKENED FIRST and crept downstairs to the kitchen, where she whipped up a batch of whole-grain muffins, squeezed orange juice and made coffee. It was a comfortable kitchen in which to work. A comfortable house. And Jackson seemed to have a comfortable life here. What if she joined him? Would she fit in? Would she be *comfortable*? The very idea frightened her. She wasn't used to comfortable. She was used to excitement, adventure, even danger and hardship.

Of course, Jackson hardly lived a normal, sedentary existence. There was adventure and excitement in his life, too. He went off to exotic places to make his documentaries—to study, to observe and to participate in environments totally unlike that of quiet, picturesque Coronado, California. And he was an expert yachtsman and naturalist, and had passed his skill along to others, had faced his own hardships and dangers.

But he always had this to come back to. His little house by the sea. His home. His comfort. Sage had a room at a lodge, and now her land, where she'd camped out a couple of times under the stars. She had nothing that could be called a permanent home, and up until now would have denied she even wanted one. She wasn't ready to settle down. She wanted to be like Grandpa Killibrew—free to do as she pleased.

Only now she wasn't so sure. There was Jackson. He had burst into her life and showed no indication of wanting to sneak back out, quietly, leaving both of them unchanged. And she didn't want him to. As uncertain as she was of where they were headed, she couldn't face the thought of cutting him out of her life or being cut out of his life after they'd resolved this mess with the paintings.

Jackson arrived in the kitchen in shorts and a T-shirt just as she was pulling the muffins out of the oven. She grinned at him. "Nice timing."

He laughed and made a show of smelling the muffins. "Aren't you handy to have around?"

"Better try them before you say anything."

"Who said I was talking about the muffins?" he murmured, putting his arms around her waist from behind. All she wore was one of his shirts, with just three buttons buttoned. She had been feeling sexy already; his touch made her feel even sexier.

Together they piled breakfast onto a tray and went out to the terrace, where there was an invigorating chill in the air. Even dressed as she was, Sage didn't mind. Every fiber of her body—of her very being—seemed alert. She couldn't ever recall feeling so alive.

They'd both agreed the muffins were delicious and it was doubtful there'd be any leftovers when the telephone rang. Jackson volunteered to answer it, and Sage, slathering her second muffin with jam, was willing to let him.

He returned in a few moments, frowning and in a sudden hurry. "I've got to go," he said, snatching another muffin. "You just take your time and relax. I'll be back as soon as I can."

Instantly suspicious, she stopped chewing. "What's up?"

"Nothing that should concern you," he said vaguely, but not sharply, and as if distracted, headed back inside.

Sage stayed put, the muffins feeling like lead in her stomach. The "should" was what got her—a judgment call. *His* judgment. As if he didn't know damn well whatever he was up to did indeed concern her. Well, heck, she thought. She hadn't told him about her sessions with Grandpa and their workable, if somewhat outrageous, plan, but he hadn't told her exactly what he and his mother had opted to do. And neither Sage nor Jackson had been able to come up with a new plan to negotiate a settlement between Bradford Killibrew and Reuben Kirk. They were fresh out of ideas, and almost out of time.

And now, more than ever, Sage didn't want to be shut out.

But she lay back, her legs stretched out and her feet propped on the chair he'd just vacated. She sipped her orange juice. Jackson might not remember, but she did: his mother had taken his car. If he wanted to go anywhere, he would have to borrow Sage's car, and there would be strings attached to that little request—namely, that she got to go along.

In a few minutes he rushed outside wearing sneakers and a pair of jeans. "I'll need to borrow your car."

"No problem," she said, dropping her feet to the ground. "I'll drive. Give me ten seconds to get dressed."

He glared at her. "Don't be a pain. I don't have time."

"By the time we're finished arguing, I could be dressed. Don't worry. I'll drive you wherever you want to go."

"I had a feeling you were going to be like this," he grumbled, but there was a smugness in his expression that instantly put her on her guard. He dug into his jean pocket and produced her set of keys, dangling them in front of her. A gleam of victory came into his eyes. "You left them upstairs. A bit of foresight on my part to swipe them out of your pant pocket, don't you think?"

Outwitted again. Sage jumped to her feet, but Jackson was already sauntering out to her car. Having dealt with his tenacious nature before, she knew better than to try arguing with him, and instead did the next best thing: she jumped on his back. Literally. Holding him around the neck, she hoisted her long legs up over his hips.

"Dammit, Kirk, you aren't going anywhere without me!"

"I'm going to parade around San Diego with a half-naked woman on my back?" He reached around behind him and grabbed a handful of her naked rear end. "Not likely."

Then he proceeded to pick her off his back like a bug and set her on a chair. The big shirt she was wearing had gone all askew, so that most of one thigh and one breast showed. Jackson inhaled deeply, obviously distracted. "Now a view like that could delay me," he said in a husky voice.

She stuck her chin up at him. "I refuse to seduce you into letting me come with you."

"It wouldn't work, anyway," he said with a wry smile. "I could make love to you right out here, in damned short order, and then still leave without you."

"Creep."

"I prefer scoundrel or rogue—not that name-calling will get you anywhere, either."

"You're shutting me out!"

His smile broadened into a grin, as sexy as any she'd seen. "Turnabout's fair play. Have *you* told me what you and Bradford have cooked up?" Bending down, he kissed the exposed part of her breast, then her throat, then her mouth. "I'll see you soon. If anything interesting happens, I'll let you know."

Pride and her skimpy attire were all that kept Sage from chasing him down the street, but as soon as he rounded the corner of the house, she was up out of her chair and racing inside. *Her* car, dammit! It would have bugged her if he'd gone off and left her in his own car, but in hers ... Well, that called for action.

She phoned for a cab, then went upstairs and pulled on some clothes. A clump of money sat on his dresser—and not Monopoly money, either. "Ha!" she exclaimed and clapped her hands together in delight. The money fit nicely into her shorts pocket.

She was out front when her taxi arrived, and taking a wild guess, she told the driver to head to the marina where Grandpa Killibrew had his boat moored. Maybe Jackson was headed there; maybe he wasn't. It was as good a bet as any.

While the driver waited at the marina, Sage ran around to Grandpa's boat, but there was no sign of life there. She called out several times before she gave up and returned to the cab. This time she gave him Reuben Kirk's address. The fare was already gigantic, but she didn't care. She'd pay with Jackson's money. It'd serve him right!

She saw her rented car *and* the Alfa Romeo in the elder Kirk's driveway, and after dismissing the driver she raced up the walkway. Shouts were coming from the back. Knowing her way around—she'd been over her map with Grandpa at least a dozen times and remembered vividly the episode with Jackson under the bougainvillea—she headed around to the terrace but automatically slowed down and grew downright stealthy as she got closer. She didn't want to barge in on a family quarrel that was none of her business.

She needn't have worried.

Grandpa Killibrew was standing perilously close to the edge of the pool with his arms flailing and his face a darker and meaner shade of violet than Jackson Kirk's eyes. Not a happy individual. Reuben Kirk was seated at one of the limestone tables with his arms folded haughtily across his chest and his head turned so that he wouldn't have to look at Grandpa, or anyone, which only seemed to infuriate his adversary more. Probably it was meant to. If Reuben Kirk and Bradford Killibrew had been friends for as long as Jackson had indicated, undoubtedly they knew how to get each other's goat.

Frances Kirk stood between them, pleading for them both to shut up. She looked elegant and sensible, but an understandable frustration had seeped into her voice. Neither man was paying her any attention. If Sage had been in her shoes, she'd have popped them both on the head with a couple of the potted plants hanging about.

She was about to reach for some red geraniums when she spied Jackson leaning against a post, as if he couldn't care less what the two older men did or said. Sage felt her own blood begin to boil. The point was he was here and he had known damn well that this little episode *did* concern her. What had he thought? That she'd just exacerbate the situation?

She reminded herself of her impulse to smash pots over heads, but of course, *she* knew she'd have talked herself out of it . . . wouldn't she?

"You're a thief and a scoundrel," Grandpa yelled.

Frances looked pained. "Bradford, *please*."

Being a Killibrew, Sage knew Frances was wasting her breath, and it was all Sage herself could do not to join the melee, Jackson or no Jackson. But she remained among the flowers and shrubs, awaiting the opportunity to reveal her own good sense—or just to pounce if the Kirks decided to gang up on Grandpa!

"Look at me, you fiend," Grandpa demanded, totally absorbed in his little drama. Reuben, of course, paid no attention. "The Blue Hill Series doesn't belong to you any more than the Mona Lisa does!"

That got Reuben Kirk. He swung around in his chair, dropping his arms from their crossed position. "You arrogant wretch, listen to you!" he yelled back, his voice still, somehow, sounding cultured. "You dare to compare yourself to Leonardo da Vinci. My, that's precious. You'll be lucky if people remember you five years from now, never mind five hundred!"

Grandpa snorted loudly, going a shade darker. "You're twisting my words, like you always do!"

Frances groaned. Hands on her hips, she glared from her long-time friend to her ex-husband. "And you both call yourselves grown men," she said, sarcastic and disgusted. "I've seen teenagers conduct more mature arguments. Be sensible, for heaven's sake. What's this ridiculous feud going to cost you? Is it *worth* it?"

No, but Sage doubted that had ever mattered.

Reuben jumped up and flew at Frances in a rage. "You've a hell of a nerve to intrude in my house and lecture *me*! After spending the night with him—"

"I spent the night on his boat, not with him," Frances cut in, exasperated. "Reuben, you can be such an ass. And what difference does it make to you where or with whom I sleep? We're not married anymore. I'm not your concern."

Sage winced, hearing the undertone of pain in Frances Kirk's seemingly reasonable words. That was all they needed—another wrinkle to this mess!

Reuben sniffed, straightening, but the anger and bitterness were still in his voice as he said, "You'd still be my wife if it hadn't been for him."

The him was Grandpa Killibrew, who'd begun to grumble to himself and pace along the edge of the pool. He wasn't looking quite as purple. He paused at Reuben's accusation but for once kept his mouth shut. He didn't need to open it; Frances had plenty to say herself.

"And Ana Luiza," she said icily, "would *she* still be your wife if it hadn't been for Bradford? No, Reuben, she'd be a tortured young woman still looking for herself, still trying to establish an identity independent from the great Reuben Kirk. She'd be miserable. Maybe she'd still be in your bed if Bradford hadn't encouraged her to be true to herself and work with her people, but where would that leave her? Where would it leave you? Even at your worst, Reuben—and God knows what an ass you can be—that's not something you'd have wanted. You're not that kind of man. But it takes a strong, independent woman to put up with you."

Reuben looked away, again folding his arms on his chest, as if that alone would prevent him from hearing things he didn't want to hear. "I'll let the facts speak for themselves."

"Bradford didn't break us up, either," Frances went on intrepidly. "If you'll recall, he did what he could to help us work out our problems. Maybe—" she sighed wistfully, her gentle eyes downcast "—maybe we should have let him." She threw up her arms and looked with despair to her son. "I told you my coming would only aggravate the problem. I'm sorry. Obviously I don't have any in-fluence over either of these . . . these boys."

"It's all right, Mother." Jackson stepped forward. His utter calm didn't impress Sage; it annoyed her. He said, "There's no need for self-recrimination. You did what you could. I'm just sorry we had to cut into old wounds."

"Maybe you ought to quit your meddling," Grandpa said, "and let your father and me fight our own battles."

Jackson looked from his mother to the cantankerous artist, but his calm expression didn't change. He refused to rise to Bradford's bait. "Why don't I drive you back to your boat—"

"I'd as soon walk," Grandpa said with a sneer.

Sage could have kicked him right into the pool. Couldn't her stubborn old grandfather see that Jackson was trying desperately to maintain his neutrality—to bring peace, for heaven's sake! She'd gotten over Jackson's trying to steal her briefcase; Grandpa could get over his breaking into his boat. But Grandpa, she was begin-ning to see, had little use for forgiveness.

"I'll drive him," Frances said briskly.

Then Reuben objected, and a fresh argument broke out. Instead of listening, Sage shook her head in disgust and took the opportunity to sneak around to the front and into the Kirk house. She wasn't sure what she hoped to find, if anything at all, but knowing her way around could come in handy at the showing *if* she got that far. The short time she'd spent there during dinner Monday night hadn't allowed her to nose around much.

In the dining room she found a couple of unused in-vitations to the Sunday showing plopped right there on the table. She almost whooped with joy. This, she thought, could be the answer to her and Grandpa's final unresolved dilemma: how to get into the showing without causing a ruckus. Neither Killibrew, of course, had been invited.

"How very fortuitous," she muttered and quickly pocketed one of the invitations, then continued her snooping.

Her curiosity was piqued by a locked door off the dining room, and she forgot the goings-on outside altogether. All the other rooms downstairs were open, adding to the house's atmosphere of airiness and welcome. This was the only locked door. And somehow she had to get in there.

But as she debated how, short of kicking in the door, a shadow fell over her, and before she could whirl around, a big hand covered her mouth and she felt herself being pulled against the hard length of a familiar body, one she had stroked and loved and felt inside her own.

"Couldn't resist a locked door, could you?" Jackson said softly against her ear. "Don't yell. Father doesn't know you're here."

When his hand lowered from her mouth, she turned around in his arms and whispered fiercely, "Scare me to death why don't you!"

He gave her a look utterly without remorse.

"Where's my grandfather?" she demanded.

"He capitulated. My mother's taking him back to his boat."

"Your father?"

"Still fuming out on the terrace."

She took a breath. "And how did you know I was here?"

"I sensed your presence," he said with a grin.

"Meaning you saw me hanging around outside. No wonder you were taking such care to appear neutral—

didn't want to lash out against Grandpa with me eavesdropping."

He frowned at her and let her go. "Did the jackass fairy come and sprinkle dust over you last night?"

"You should know. You were with me all night."

A warmth came into his eyes as he remembered, but it vanished as he shook his head. "You're about as impossible to reason with as your grandfather."

"The words of a neutral party!"

That almost broke his composure. "Dammit—" he started but cut himself off with a hiss. He took a deep, calming breath. "You're just mad because you don't like being caught."

"I am mad," she snapped back, articulating each word with emphasis, "because you knew what was going on here and didn't tell me. You wanted me to sit around stuffing myself with muffins! Who called? Your father?"

"My mother," he replied stiffly. "Bradford and my father were at each other's throats, and she thought I might be of some help. At least I could break them up if things got out of hand."

"Did she ask you not to bring me?"

"No."

"Then it was your idea."

"Things were volatile enough without . . ." He didn't finish.

But Sage was persistent. "Without what?"

"All right, dammit. Without throwing fuel on their fire. Sage, you're not neutral, and even if you were, you can't help stirring things up. It's in your nature. You don't have a pacifying influence on people. That's not good or bad, it's just you."

"So I'm a hothead."

He gave her his half smile. "Let's just say you're a woman of strong convictions and you compel other people to examine their own convictions, to dig in their heels on points of honor. Even if you hadn't said a word, Sage, you'd have stirred up those two even more—not that I had much more success." He sighed and changed the subject. "How did you get here?"

"Cab." Not mollified yet, she bit off the word.

"I should have guessed. You're a determined woman, aren't you? That must have cost you a fortune."

"No, it cost you." The thought of her touch of "foresight" eased her anger somewhat. "You swiped my car, I swiped the money you left on the bureau."

"I did not 'swipe' your car!" He was struggling to keep his voice down. "I merely borrowed it. You'll get the damned thing back. But my money..."

"Gone with the wind," she said airily. Ahh, vengeance.

He looked as if he wanted to throttle her, but instead he said through clenched teeth, "Let me get you out of here before I give up and haul you out to my father. He's in the worst mood I've ever seen him in. He'd probably have you thrown in jail for trespassing, which just might be the best place for you!"

She imitated one of Grandpa Killibrew's snorts of disgust.

"You have no idea of the patience I'm exercising," Jackson said, his teeth clenched even more tightly. He grabbed her wrist. She tried to pull away, but he held on. Knowing how angry she'd been only seconds ago, how volatile, she decided it might be prudent to let the man have his way this once. Besides, she had no desire whatsoever to confront Reuben Kirk, in a good mood or bad. With a show of cooperation, if not meekness, she permitted Jackson to lead her out of the house to her rented car. He shoved her into the driver's seat, shut the door and handed her the keys through the open window.

"Go where you please," he said, "do as you please. I'll catch up with you at some point."

She looked at him, her hands on the steering wheel, unsure of just what his anger might mean. Had she gone too far this time? "Would you like me to check back into the Hotel Del?"

He grunted. "Not if you're paying for the room with my money."

With that he turned and started to walk away, cock-ily, so that she knew he was goading her deliberately. She grabbed what was left of his money—almost two hundred dollars, she realized with a jolt—and wadded it up nice and tight. Then she pitched it at him. The wad hit him smack in the middle of the back. He whipped around and started to lunge toward her, but she had the car started and in gear before he could get to her throat.

"All's fair in love and war," she said with a mocking smile as she backed down the driveway. "Ta-ta."

He swooped down and snatched up the money, then glared at her with a wild, unpredictable expression. She had visions of him leaping onto her car hood. Instead, he gave her the sexiest of grins and blew her a kiss that almost made her stop the car and jump into his arms.

Of course, she thought, that was what he wanted. If he kept her totally off balance, then she wouldn't inter-fere and help her grandfather get back his paintings. She wouldn't "stir things up." Well, she'd interfere, anyway. And if she stirred things up, then fine. So long as this feud between Reuben and her grandfather ended. She had other things to think about now. What was happening between her and Jackson, for one.

Then she thought with a sudden rush of panic, *What have I done?*

Glancing in the rearview mirror at his motionless figure, she could only wonder...and hope. She didn't want this man thinking she was a jackass, thinking she was a thoughtless troublemaker. She didn't want him stalking angrily out of her life.

"Not now," she breathed, emotions swelling inside her. "Not ever."

She was in love with him, she realized, her heart thudding painfully. Not sexually infatuated, not just smitten, but in love. And with *him*—the man, just as he was, not some romanticized idea of him.

It wasn't an impulsive love, either. Instead, it was as if this was the man she'd been waiting for all her life.

She smiled to herself, relieved by knowing where her emotions stood, frightened by where they might lead her. My rogue, she thought. Now what would Auntie Killibrew say to that?

SHE FOUND HER GRANDFATHER in a pensive mood as he paced the deck of his dilapidated boat. "He's a bitter, bitter man, Reuben is," he said, shaking his head with a heavy sigh. "I don't know what to say to him."

"Perhaps it's best you don't say anything." Sage came around and leaned against the gunnel, where Grandpa was looking out at the Pacific. The mist had burned off, revealing a gloriously blue sky; she could see how the San Diego climate could become habit-forming.

Almost to himself Grandpa said, "I have to; he's my friend."

"What—*still?*"

He looked at her as if she'd gone daft. "Well, of course."

"I thought he was a wretch and a fiend and all sorts of nasty things!" She groaned at this new twist in her grandfather's logic. Just when she'd thought she had him and his dilemma all figured out! "I thought you were furious with him."

"He is, and I am"

"But he's your friend," she said.

"That's right." He seemed relieved she'd finally seen what he figured had been obvious all along.

It was all Sage could do to maintain some semblance of patience. "Then why go through all this? Why risk your friendship? Why not understand that the man's been through an emotional hell, of his own making or not, and . . . and . . ." Her voice had been increasing in volume, and as she threw up her hands, she yelled, "And *give up?*"

He shrugged. "Because I want my paintings back, as we agreed. I'll only go so far. But I'm acting out of honor. Necessity, even. Reuben's motivated only by his own bitterness, his own blindness to anyone's pain but his own. He's being selfish, and maybe I can help him see that and mend his ways." He heaved another sigh and came and stood beside her. "Then again, maybe not. He wasn't always like this, Sage. Reuben Kirk has a fine sense of humor, he's generous, thoughtful . . . I don't know. Perhaps focusing his anger on me saves him from facing things in himself he's not ready to face."

Sage hadn't expected such philosophizing, such empathy, from her grandfather. It was simpler to deal with his rages. "Look, Grandpa, it doesn't matter a whole lot whether or not you consider Reuben Kirk a friend. He obviously doesn't consider you one, and if you try to steal the paintings—"

"If I take back what's rightfully mine!"

"You know what I mean." But the outburst reassured her. Pensive though he was, Grandpa hadn't gone maudlin on her. "He could have you arrested. Maybe not morally, but in the eyes of the law, the Blue Hill Series belongs to Reuben Kirk."

Grandpa waved a bony arm, dismissing her worries. "We've been through this a thousand times. Reuben wouldn't *dare* have me arrested. Think of the publicity! The humiliation when people find out what a nefarious lout he's been!"

It was Sage's turn to sigh. "Grandpa, Reuben is as convinced he's right as you are. Jackson says he will call the police if—"

"Bah!"

"He's your friend, too."

"He's a pain in the neck is what he is!" The spark was back, the pensiveness gone. "I'm surprised he hasn't stolen the paintings himself, just to keep Reuben and me from having this thing out."

Not a bad idea, Sage thought. "Jackson would never do anything like that."

"He's as crazy as you are, m'girl—acts before he thinks, most of the time. I wouldn't put anything past him. Maybe that's why you two have hit it off so well: you're so much alike."

"Grandpa," she said sternly, "you can just never mind Jackson Kirk and me. What is or isn't going on between us has nothing whatever to do with you. I haven't betrayed your trust, and Jackson—All I'm saying is I believe he's at least trying to remain neutral. He just wants this thing to end peacefully. So do I, but I'm willing to help you get your paintings back if push comes to shove. I can't be neutral, I guess. But if you just gave Jackson a chance..."

"Jackson Kirk is trying to protect his father," Grandpa said stubbornly, his beady eyes alive with the certainty of his convictions. "You mark my words. He doesn't want Reuben Kirk to look like a damn fool."

Sage wanted to scream. "I might as well be talking to a mule," she muttered. "What about Frances Kirk?"

Grandpa lifted his lean shoulders in a guileless shrug, as if the last thing he could possibly be was mule-headed. "She talked me into going to see Reuben this morning, just as one last gesture of good faith. I was reluctant, as you can imagine, and it was one hell of a waste of time. We argued—"

"I was there," Sage said.

"You were? Ha!" His piercing blue eyes lit up. "Good for you! Heard everything did you?"

"Enough." She studied him as a slight sea breeze floated through her hair, and she thought back to her tiptoeing through Reuben Kirk's house and finding the invitation, the locked door, Jackson Kirk. Perhaps this time it was her turn to keep her mouth shut, but how could she hold out on her grandfather at this stage? After all their strategy sessions? After the twenty years of separation? Besides, somehow she felt her news might keep him from doing anything impetuous—or, worse, going ahead without her. Given his current mood, she wouldn't put anything past him. "Grandpa, I'm not sure I should be telling you this...."

"Spit it out, m'girl."

She hesitated, then plunged ahead. "I think I may have located where Reuben Kirk is keeping the paintings...and I managed to get my hands on an invitation to the showing."

When she pulled out the blank invitation, a wide smile spread across Grandpa's leathery face, and there was a roguish wickedness to the gleam in his eyes. "Well, I'll be damned. There's no doubt about it, Sage m'girl, you're a Killibrew—and the Kirks had best be watching out for the two of us!"

"Frankly," she said, "I hope they're not."

12

HIS ALFA ROMEO WAS in his Coronado driveway, but there was no sign of Jackson as Sage prowled through the house, feeling her excitement build at the thought of seeing him again. At what she had planned for when she did see him. She was an optimist: he wouldn't be mad at her.

First, of course, she had to find him.

Her frustration mounting, she headed out back, but the terrace was as quiet and empty as the house. Maybe he'd gone jogging. Or had work to do. Damn, she thought. That didn't fit into her plan.

Then she spied him sprawled in the rope hammock in the secluded garden off the terrace. One tanned arm was crooked over his face as he slept. She smiled to herself. So last night had finally caught up with him, she thought with a little thrill, walking silently over to him.

"Are you awake?" she whispered.

He didn't move a muscle. From under his arm he muttered, "No, go away."

A heck of a greeting, considering her own anticipation. Maybe he was in a sleeplike trance. "It's me," she said, "Sage."

"Mmm, I'm dreaming about you."

"Then does that explain this?" she asked, boldly brushing her fingertips across the telltale bulge in his jeans.

He moved his arm to reveal one violet eye. "That's thin ice you're treading on, you know."

"Is it? Feels more like a man's—"

"Watch it."

She grinned, smelling the sweetness of the flowers in the air and feeling her body begin to ache with the now familiar need, the want. "Isn't the real me better than a dream?"

"I don't know." The single eye roved over her, spreading the ache. "In my dream you don't steal money and you don't plot with your grandfather."

"What do I do?"

"You make love—tirelessly."

"My, my. Where's your mother?"

"My *mother*? Good God, what timing. She's gone to stay with a friend in Point Loma. She wangled an invitation from Father to the showing on Sunday, and Bradford, of course, tried to get it off her. How he thinks he could pass for my mother I don't know." Jackson peered at her suspiciously. "Why do you ask?"

"Simple curiosity," she lied.

"Nothing is ever simple with you, Sage Killibrew."

She'd learned to take such remarks as compliments. "How would you like me to dump you out of this hammock?"

"You wouldn't dare." His arm dropped completely from his face, revealing two violet eyes that were suddenly very alert.

"Wouldn't I?"

And before he could so much as grab the hammock for support, she was heaving it up to one side, toppling him onto the ground. Yelling "You little witch," as the hammock swung violently, he grabbed her by the waist and pulled her with him. They landed in a heap, Sage on top. It wasn't exactly what she'd planned but close enough.

With a growl he rolled onto his back, but she managed to stay on top of him, straddling his hips. Every inch of him was as hard and sexy as any man she'd ever dreamed about. Her heart hammered in anticipation of what she intended to have happen next. She grinned down at him and picked a few blades of grass from his lips and cheek. "Am I horrible?"

"Yes," he said, his annoyance totally feigned, "horrible."

"I suppose that was a rude awakening from your dream?"

He gave her a dry look. "You've no idea."

She leaned over, pressing herself on his stomach and chest, and gently blew a lock of dark hair from his eyes. "Does that mean my plan's doomed to failure?"

"Oh, God, not another plan."

"Ah, but what a plan this is."

"Does it involve moving?" he asked skeptically.

"In a certain sense."

He gave a long-suffering sigh. "Sage, out with it. Tell me your plan and—"

"I can't tell you."

His eyes narrowed. "More secrets?"

"Uh-uh, I have to show you."

"Good God." He heaved another sigh. "All right, all right, show me."

She sat up, still straddling him, and edged down his hips to his thighs. His brows furrowed as he watched her with growing consternation, as if he couldn't quite fathom what she was up to. She grinned innocently and shrugged her shoulders, as if she couldn't, either. Then she unbuttoned his jeans, unzipped them and slowly eased them and his underpants down to his thighs.

Jackson, she noticed, didn't protest. In fact, he cooperated.

When his manhood sprang free from the confining garments, she looked at him with a raised brow. "I guess my plan isn't doomed to failure after all."

He didn't say a word but lay very still, waiting to see what she'd do next. Raising herself slightly, her knees still on the grass on either side of his hips, she lifted her skirt—and saw the delighted surprise in his eyes when he realized she wasn't wearing underpants.

"Dealt with that little plot problem while I was in the car," she said proudly.

He gave a low growl of a laugh. "You *are* a witch."

"And half your dream woman. I may 'steal' money, and my grandfather and I may have our secret plans, but I also make love—tirelessly."

With that she eased herself down onto him, pulling him inside her and gasping at the sweet, expected thrill of it. Jackson remained very still. Then she realized he was waiting for her to make the first move, to set the pace...and she did, willingly, rocking her hips back and forth until he couldn't stand it anymore and moaned aloud, grabbing her hips. She settled back down on his stomach and chest and pulled her hips up slightly, then plunged them down rapidly, over and over and over again, making him thrust deeper into her. The contact dizzied her. She pushed herself off his chest once more, slowing the pace as she moved over his hips in tantalizing circles, and she saw him grimacing with want. Finally he shuddered, pressing her down onto him, deeper, harder. She could feel her breasts straining against the fabric of her bra and blouse and her insides filling with an ache that screamed to be alleviated.

She cried out his name and felt herself bursting, the ache focused on her hot core, peaking...and then slowly, with a precious agony, easing.

Just as she wanted to collapse on him, Jackson threw both arms around her waist and pulled her against him, holding her there as he rocked and thrust madly inside her, finding his own peak, his own release.

Then they both collapsed.

After a long while he stroked her hair and kissed her on the nose, the cheek, the mouth. "Am I awake now?" he asked.

She smiled at him. "You were awake before. Just admit it, Kirk, I'm as good as the woman of your dreams."

"As good? Darlin', you're better. Even as I lay in that hammock hoping you'd come, imagining all sorts of things, I never once imagined you dumping me onto the grass and seducing me. Slipping your underpants off in the car, for heaven's sake."

"A question of logistics," she replied, a glint in her eye.

"You had it planned to that degree?"

"I didn't know you'd be in the hammock, of course, but, well, I try to leave as little to chance as possible." She was having a grand time, lying in the grass, with the flowers and shrubs all around them, just being with him. "Now tell me, what kind of imaginings?"

"I figured I'd do the seducing."

"Ahh."

Then he rolled over on top of her and did what he'd imagined.

THEY MADE DINNER for Jackson's mother that evening, a simple meal of grilled salmon, rice pilaf, salad, plenty of

good wine and a fruit sorbet for dessert. Sage had showered and put on one of her new skirts and tops, and she
felt fresh and clean and, well, loved, she admitted silently as they retired to the living room with coffee. She'd
made the coffee from water-processed decaffeinated
beans she'd ground herself. She'd done the shopping
alone so that she could think, although she hadn't. She'd
found her way around the shops and grocery store, just
delighted to be doing what she was doing. She absorbed
herself in the moment, in the little things, and didn't
worry about the big ones—the quarrel over the Blue Hill
Series, the secret plan she and her grandfather had de-
vised, what would become of her and Jackson. Picking
out coffee beans and salmon, she just relished being in
love. And it was a grand feeling.

"Today was a disaster," Frances said, rousing Sage
from her thoughts. "I'm sorry I wasn't more help."

By an unspoken mutual agreement, they hadn't
brought up the feud during the dinner, discussing more
conventional subjects instead, like the weather and pol-
itics, on which, fortunately, they agreed. Sage had told
Frances a bit about her work; Frances returned the fa-
vor. Jackson had been content to let the conversation
drift along, satisfied, it seemed, that Sage and his mother
were getting along so well—unlike Sage and his father.

Seated on the couch next to Sage, Jackson, showered
and fresh-smelling, leaned forward. "Don't be sorry,
Mother," he said. "We've all had our stab at this—without success."

Frances made a little noise of pure irritation. "Reuben's being such an ass, but Bradford should never have
agreed to help Ana like that. He should have guessed
what would happen and instead encouraged Ana to face
Reuben and whatever problems they were having in-

stead of hiding. Of course, I can understand that urge."
She bit her lip suddenly, looking down at her untouched
cup of coffee. "Reuben can be a difficult man to face with
something he doesn't want to hear."

A warmth and sadness came into Jackson's eyes that
made him look anything but a rogue. "Mother..."

But Frances chased away her melancholy with a quick
smile. "He must have felt terribly used—as if Bradford
and Ana were playing a cruel joke on him, which, of
course, wasn't the case at all. Ana's so idealistic, so very
devoted to that home, and Bradford, well, you know
Bradford Killibrew and his causes. He never has a penny
in his pocket, and he gets so wrapped up in what he's
supporting it just never occurs to him that someone
might be offended by his tactics, especially a good friend
like Reuben. But this time he went a bit too far." She
shook her head in frustration. "If only they each could
see the other's side!"

"They think they can," Jackson put in dryly.

"Yes, but only from their own perspective. Obviously
there's no point in trying to tell them that. We've all tried,
and even if they did listen, I'm not sure it would resolve
this mess about the paintings. Reuben could just keep his
end of the deal he made with Bradford, but he's in this
too deeply now; he'll need some face-saving gesture. It
won't do to have it seem Bradford was totally in the
right."

Sage poured herself some coffee from the tray on the
cherry table in front of her, then sat back. "I agree, but
what's this about my grandfather and his causes? I don't
understand."

Frances gave an incredulous laugh. "You mean you
don't know?"

Sage shook her head, eyeing Jackson, suspecting this might be just one more little something he'd neglected to tell her. But he showed no sign of surprise or guilt. Instead, he said matter-of-factly, "I don't know what Sage and Bradford have been talking about, but she and I haven't spent a great deal of time going into detail about what her grandfather's been up to the last twenty years."

"No, I don't suppose you have," Frances replied, leaving it at that. She was an intelligent woman; she could guess what was going on. "And I can certainly see why Bradford would never have told you. Again, it just wouldn't occur to him. He sins more by omission than commission, not that there's any false humility in the man—not much humility whatsoever, I should say. In any case, twenty years ago Bradford Killibrew came to South America a fairly wealthy man, even by U.S. standards. He and Reuben and I became friends right away, he took up painting and we all thought he'd live a comfortable, routine sort of existence."

"Grandpa Killibrew *never* lived a comfortable, routine existence, even when he was running the family company," Sage said. "It's just not the Killibrew way."

Jackson gave her a look but said nothing.

Frances drank some coffee. "So we discovered. We never anticipated he'd do much with his painting, and consequently didn't take it very seriously, but soon it became quite evident *he* was serious. We didn't see much of his work in those early years; he was very secretive. But he went at it at a feverish pace and, in the meantime, started donating funds here and there to various charities and enterprises doing what he considered good works, mostly dealing with human resources and the environment. He lived simply and bugged all his wealthy friends to 'spring loose some cash,' as he would delicately put it, for one cause or another. Well, it wasn't too, too long before he was flat broke, and that forced him to begin showing his work and developing his reputation as an artist. I'm not sure he would have done a thing with his work if he hadn't needed the money. He's still picky about what he sells and to whom. Reuben and I purchased a number of his works, but I don't think he's ever wanted either of us to have the Blue Hill Series. As he told me last night in his blunt but kind way, it just wasn't meant for us."

"Then he never should have risked selling it like that," Sage complained, still adjusting to her crusty grandfather in the role of miniphilanthropist. She'd always considered him plain stingy.

Frances shrugged. "At the time, he didn't consider it a risk."

Sage swallowed some coffee, confused and frustrated. "This doesn't get any easier, does it?"

"No, I'm afraid it doesn't," Frances agreed grimly. "And if we don't come up with *something* before Sunday, I don't even want to imagine what might happen. Unfortunately, there's not much I can do."

"There's not much any of us can do," Jackson said.

Frances nodded, setting down her coffee cup and rising. "I suppose you're right. I don't know, maybe it would be best if we just kept quiet and let those two go at it. Unless I get a sudden inspiration, that's what I'm inclined to do. Well, I should be going." She smiled warmly. "See you on Sunday, if not sooner."

After his mother left, Jackson settled back down on the couch with Sage, and together they polished off the last of the wine. "You're not going to tell me what you and your grandfather have planned for Sunday, are you?" he asked.

Sage sipped some wine and didn't meet his penetrating gaze. "A last resort."

"Ahh."

"Don't." She sighed. "Please don't ask me questions I can't answer."

"Well, whatever you two have cooked up," he said, leaning closer, his breath smelling of wine and coffee and desire, "I think I can talk Father into just throwing Bradford into jail."

"And me?"

He gave her his rogue's smile. "You he'll just have to leave to me."

SAGE AWOKE to the sun streaming through the window and the feeling that everything was right in her world. Last night she had discovered, been shown, what their center was, what could hold her and Jackson together and provide some stability for their relationship. Yes, they were a lot alike, and when they disagreed, there'd be fireworks—but never violence, never anything that would threaten the foundation of who and what they were together. Yes, there was a lot of energy between them. Individually, they were hard to keep down; together, impossible. They were tempestuous and stubborn and impulsive, but Sage somehow knew those were qualities that ultimately would pull them together, not apart . . . because they had their center. And it was so simple to define she felt silly for not having seen it sooner. Last night, all night, she'd felt the passion that was between them, the love, the caring, the willingness to do anything for each other—and *that* was their center. For them it would be enough.

As she stretched, waking up, she was just so sure of it.

Then, swinging one arm onto Jackson's side of the bed, she felt nothing but pillows and tangled sheets and bolted upright, instantly alert. Perhaps because they *were* so much alike, she sensed immediately that something was wrong. But in a normal voice she called, "Jackson?"

There was no answer in the still house.

"Jackson?" Louder this time, the foreboding beginning to show.

Again no answer.

She leaped out of bed. "*Jackson!*"

It was a proper bellow, but still there was no answer. She started out of the room, to yell downstairs, but her eye caught a scrap of paper on his bureau. She seized it in fury. He'd written in a black scrawl: "Had some things to do; didn't want to wake you. See you tonight. Jackson."

"My eye," she muttered in disgust.

He was up to something. Dammit, she knew he was! He'd gone solo. Plotting his own strategy for tomorrow...without her.

Well, her inner voice countered, *isn't that what you've done to him?*

But that was different; Bradford Killibrew was the grandfather she hadn't seen in twenty years. There were mitigating circumstances. Her sneakiness was justified!

Her inner voice was adamant. *Reuben Kirk is Jackson's father, and Bradford Killibrew is his friend—and you're his lover. He wants peace, and he'll do what he has to do to get it. And you'll just have to understand.*

Waiting quietly in the sidelines—being that kind of understanding—wasn't Sage's style. It was too passive. She wanted to do something. She wanted to *act.*

What she wanted to do, she admitted, was kick something, but since her feet were bare, she satisfied herself by crumpling the note and pelting it across the room.

Unfortunately, that wasn't very satisfying at all.

She showered and got dressed and, skipping breakfast, headed out to La Jolla. She whipped around Reuben's place. No Alfa Romeo in sight. And at the marina Grandpa was alone, fishing. Maybe, she thought, Jackson's "things to do" didn't involve the Kirk-Killibrew feud.

Ha!

"Don't you ever work?" she asked her grandfather irritably.

He turned around, a grin on his weathered face, ignoring her grumpy mood completely. "Well, good morning! I was hoping you'd turn up. I've been doing some thinking. Had lunch yet?"

"I haven't had breakfast yet."

"That's no way to live." Shaking his head, he put down his rod and headed below, grumbling about young people and the kind of schedules they kept, how they missed the best part of the day. It was all of ten-fifteen. In just minutes he was back with a cheese sandwich, a tall glass of orange juice, and just a glass of iced tea for himself. Half breakfast, half lunch. Sage didn't complain.

"Where's your Jackson fellow?" he asked.

She shrugged, occupying one of the decrepit deck chairs. She drank some juice and eyed the sandwich. The cheese was a bit dry around the edges. Leave it to Grandpa not to waste a morsel. "He had some things to do today."

"Good, that means you won't be tempted to go running off to him." He plopped into the other chair and squinted in the sunshine. "I've been wondering if disrupting Reuben's showing tomorrow is the wisest course of action."

"Really?" She couldn't believe it! Had he gone sane on her? "You mean you'll sacrifice the Blue Hill Series for the sake of friendship and—"

"No," Grandpa interrupted, scoffing. He folded his hands across his lean middle. "I mean I think we should act sooner."

Oh, dear, Sage thought, her inner voice telling her she should make tracks for Colorado, and now. This whole damned business was getting impossible. "Sooner," she repeated dully.

"Today."

"Why?"

"At first I reckoned Reuben'd be more likely to expect me to make my move today, before the showing, but after yesterday I'm guessing he knows I plan to wait until tomorrow. He'll be off his guard today. And if I were being nice about it," he went on, stretching out and gulping down some tea with a look of smug satisfaction, "I'd have to say robbing the wretch today would save him some humiliation tomorrow."

"No, it wouldn't," Sage countered. "He'd have to cancel the showing or, worse, have guests appear and have nothing for them to view. Whatever you do, Grandpa, Reuben Kirk will be humiliated."

That prospect didn't seem to bother him. "Guess so, but that's his problem. He should have kept his end of the bargain."

"Yes, yes," Sage said impatiently, tired of hearing the same old refrain. Neither he nor Reuben Kirk had budged an inch! And what good was Jackson? He'd left her to cope alone. "Well, I'm not up to being a thief today, however righteous a thief. And our plans are set for tomorrow, and after all the trouble I went to sneak that invitation—"

"If we moved today . . ."

"Grandpa, we *can't!*"

His beady eyes narrowed. "Why not? Whose side are you on, Sage?" He grunted, stretching out his long thin legs. "Oh, I see. You want to delay this as long as possible so you can try to talk me out of it. Well, there'll be none of that. Either you're with me—"

"Or I'm against you?"

"No, or you're out of here. I don't want you helping me if it's against your principles—or your own interests."

By that she knew he meant Jackson. She kept quiet.

"As I've said, you won't be involved with the actual taking of the paintings; all you have to do is set me up."

"Aiding and abetting."

"Then don't. Go on back to your Jackson and forget me."

"You know I can't do that."

"With you or without you, I'll get my paintings back."

He smacked his lips together, his mouth in a straight, stubborn line, and Sage's heart went out to him. Reuben Kirk had done him wrong. Perhaps there'd been mitigating circumstances, but still, to sell a person's work, to invade the private domain of an artist, wasn't right. The Blue Hill Series, only rumored to exist in art circles, was nearest and dearest to Grandpa's heart. That was something Reuben Kirk had to know, was, in fact, probably delighted about. It made his vengeance that much sweeter. And yet as an artist himself, he should have realized, in Sage's opinion, that his "punishment" didn't fit the crime.

"Of course I'll help you," she said wearily, "but I still think tomorrow's our best bet. It's what we've planned for, and if we should fail today, well, there wouldn't be any chance tomorrow."

"Bah! Oh, all right, I suppose you have a point." He heaved his shoulders in an awkward movement. "It was just one of those crazy thoughts I get when I'm fishing, I guess. Go on, eat your sandwich."

She did, and then he got her a fishing pole and a ratty hat and they sat out on the deck together. They didn't talk much, and they didn't catch anything. But that didn't matter. She felt as if they were making up for the times they'd missed, the quiet mornings they could have spent fishing when she was a girl.

Then it occurred to her that Bradford Killibrew had never done any fishing when he'd been in Portsmouth, running a demanding company. There hadn't been time. Perhaps that was one thing he'd found—time. And in that time he'd found himself . . . and the need to paint.

When she got back to Coronado, there was still no Jackson. She phoned Juniper—she and Cal were, as she put it, elbow-deep in goo and gunk in the dining room— and told her what was going on. Being a take-charge type, Juniper naturally wanted to fly out and negotiate a settlement herself, but Sage discouraged her.

"Don't do anything crazy," Juniper warned.

"I won't."

"Yeah, well, just in case, I'll have bail money ready."

Sage laughed. "Such faith."

But as she ate supper out on the terrace, she thought it wasn't such a bad idea after all. She had gotten Grandpa to promise not to act on impulse tomorrow but, once he was inside the house, to wait and see what Reuben Kirk did...to give him, in short, that one last chance.

Knowing Reuben, he'd take the highest bid for the Blue Hill Series and be done with it.

Knowing Grandpa, even if Reuben did throw him some kind of bone and act on his last chance, it wouldn't be good enough.

Of course, not much of anything was likely to happen tomorrow if Sage didn't do her part. The invitation would get her past the private security guards hired for the occasion, but there still remained other sticky logistical problems—namely, Jackson and Reuben Kirk. Neither was a fool, and both could have her escorted off the property. And undoubtedly would.

A problem, she decided, for tomorrow. In other words, she had no choice but to wing it.

Jackson turned up just after sunset. She was at the dining room table, playing solitaire. He pulled out a chair and sat kitty-corner from her, and she had to struggle to keep her hands steady and her eyes on the cards. His presence filled the room. She itched to touch him but resisted. She was still, of course, profoundly annoyed with him.

"How were 'things'?" she asked snidely.

He shrugged those wonderful shoulders of his and looked utterly guileless. "Okay, I guess. Busy day. Your red seven plays on the black eight."

"I know that."

"Grumpy, aren't you?"

"I've been nursing a grudge against you all day."

"I knew I could count on an honest answer from you." Amusement twinkled in his violet eyes, soft in the evening light, and his straight, sexy mouth twitched. She wished she wouldn't always notice such things. "You aren't one to hide your feelings. You speak right up. I like that. Shows I don't intimidate you."

She snorted at the very idea. "Hardly. Are you going to tell me what you've been up to?"

"No."

"Already made up your mind about that, huh?" She flipped another card, which played on an ace and opened up a series of subsequent plays. "I figured I could count on you to be open and honest with me."

"I *can't* tell you, Sage," he said simply.

"As Grandpa would say, 'bah.'"

"The black jack plays—"

"On the red queen, which plays on the black king. This is *solitaire*, Kirk."

"And you don't want any help."

He didn't expect an answer, but she gave one, anyway. "Right."

"You're going to lose, no matter what you do or what I say."

"It's the playing that counts, not the winning."

"Isn't it, though." He leaned back in his chair, watching silently as she finished her game. She lost for lack of the four of hearts. Standing, Jackson flipped over the last card on the seventh pile, which she'd been unable to get to. There was the four of hearts. "Sometimes no matter how hard you try," he said, drawing her eyes to his, "no matter what you do or how much you plan, there are things you just can't help."

"I knew the four of hearts was going to be a problem early on," she told him.

"And what difference did knowing make? None."

She could feel her brow furrow in thought as she looked up at him. "It was just a matter of how the cards lay, of luck."

"That's my point exactly. Nothing you could have done, no amount of planning, could have uncovered that four of hearts. You were stuck with it, and you knew you were doomed almost from the beginning."

"But I stuck it out, anyway," she said.

He smiled then, that enigmatic half smile that he must know by now drove her wild. "You're a Killibrew, aren't you?"

"Are you trying to tell me something, something that doesn't have anything to do with this stupid card game?"

"Just that you and your grandfather may find yourselves with a few cards you can't get to, no matter how hard you've planned, or how sneaky you think you are."

And he gathered the cards, shuffled them and set them down in front of her. Then he turned without a word and walked away. She could hear his footsteps on the stairs. He was giving her a choice: she could follow him . . . or not.

Which wasn't a choice at all. She tucked the cards in her pocket and followed. To her surprise they managed to make it through one game of gin rummy on his big bed before giving in to raging hormones.

"I'm sorry I can't tell you about today," he whispered between kisses.

"I'm sorry I can't tell you what Grandpa and I have planned," she whispered back.

"Do you trust me?"

"No."

He laughed huskily, rolling on top of her. "You're a liar, Sage. You know damned well I wouldn't do anything to hurt you or your grandfather. I trust you, you know."

"Ha!"

"I do," he protested, slipping his hands under her shirt. "I trust you to do something tomorrow that's going to irritate the hell out of me."

"Kirk—"

He unclasped her bra and brought his mouth down to one breast. "Let's not worry about our secrets now. Love me tonight, Sage," he said, breathing against her straining nipple. "It's all I ask...all I'll ever want from you. Just love me, darlin'."

Her throat was tight with desire, and the only way she could answer was to gently press his mouth to her breast. It was enough.

13

"I SUPPOSE there's no chance you'd tell me the truth if I asked you what you were going to do while I'm at the showing," Jackson said early the next afternoon. They were in his bedroom, a languid morning behind them. He was dressing. His tan linen suit hugged exactly where and what it should and looked smart, stylish but not quite as flashy as his violet jacket. He was tying his tie in the mirror.

Stretched out on the bed, Sage watched him with interest as she tried to look as nonchalant as possible. All morning she'd had to squelch attacks of guilt and panic, and to resist telling him all about Grandpa Killibrew's Plan D . . . and her hand in devising it. "You look terrific in a suit," she told him. "Absolutely devastating. I think it's the scar. Of course, I know it's the man, not the body, that counts, but luckily you have both personality and good looks. You know, all those wonderful heroic qualities. Kindness, intelligence, sensitivity, great thighs . . ."

"The ability to read a crazy nut's mind," he finished, scowling over his shoulder at her. "You're not answering me."

"You can tell a lot from a man's thighs. Did you ask a question?"

"I'm giving you the opportunity to talk so I won't have to ask and—damn!" He'd messed up his tie and had to redo it.

Sage grinned and jumped off the bed. Grabbing him from behind, she kissed him lightly on the neck. "I'm going out for a quick jog on the beach—need to clear my mind. Have fun. Tell your pop hi for me."

She dodged away before he could tie her to the bedpost and interrogate her. As she ran down the stairs, her heart already pounding, she heard him bellow, "Sage!"

Plan D undoubtedly had its flaws, but she wondered if she'd ever get the chance to put it into operation. Jackson was obviously suspicious—in his position she would be, too—and if his suspicions got the better of him and he locked her in the bathroom, that would be the end of any scheme she and Grandpa Killibrew had.

But she got downstairs unscathed and ducked into his study, feeling both panic and exhilaration creeping through her, attacking her nerves. She pulled out the periwinkle knit dress she'd already stashed in the supply closet. She'd wasted a lot of time watching Jackson dress but felt she had to look as innocent as possible, to wait for the precise moment to make her exit. But that left her with damn little time. She tugged the dress on, slipped into sandals and, not bothering with hair or face, left her discarded clothes in a heap on the floor and dashed outside.

Taking her rented car was out of the question. Reuben had probably noted the plate number and suggested the guards firebomb it should it turn up in his driveway. Jackson's Alfa Romeo, however, was unlocked. Glancing all around her, looking and feeling guilty, Sage ducked into the back seat and covered herself with his car blanket. Then she tried to melt into the floor. Being as tall as she was, it wasn't easy. Also, she didn't want to wrinkle her dress. At least it was knit.

She was stiff in just the few minutes before Jackson climbed into the car. The ride to La Jolla was going to be torture, and she supposed she would endure such discomfort, not to mention tension, for no one but Grandpa Killibrew. Jackson had a temper every bit as volatile as her own. If *she* found someone hiding in the back of *her* car, there was no telling what she'd do, but she knew she wouldn't be calm or nice about it.

When they were out on the Bay Bridge—she could feel the change in the ride—she began to relax and used her powers of concentration and yoga breathing to ease the pain of being curled up in the back of an Alfa Romeo.

"I wish San Diego had more potholes," Jackson said, unperturbed. "I'd hit every one I could."

She went rigid. But no. He wasn't talking to her; he was talking to himself.

"I'd love to bump your beautiful behind up so high you'd bang your head on the ceiling. Might knock some sense into you."

Damn, she thought grimly. He was talking to her, all right. He'd made much more interesting references to her beautiful behind during the night.

"Just how the hell dumb do you think I am?" he asked matter-of-factly.

"I was hoping for unobservant," she said through the blanket, "not dumb."

He made a noise that sounded something like a growl. "You might as well climb up front."

She wasn't sure she wanted to, but there was no point in staying scrunched up in the back seat—her back and legs and knees and elbows hurt. Her hair was full of static electricity when she pulled the blanket off, and she had to admit she felt somewhat foolish. Jackson didn't help matters. He said dryly, "You look sexy as hell in that dress—your cat burglar outfit?"

"Will you stop?" She climbed into the front seat and plopped down, her hair sticking out everywhere. "You're not going to make this easy, are you?"

"Not likely."

They were on the freeway now, cruising fast toward La Jolla. "What are you going to do with me?"

"I haven't decided yet."

She took a breath, irritated with herself, with him, with Grandpa Killibrew for ever getting her into this mess. If not for his crazy telegram, she'd be in Colorado with no idea what she was missing. "Grandpa's expecting me to sneak him in, you know. If I don't, well, God knows what he'll do. Jackson, I'm not helping him to hurt your father or to sneak around your back, I'm helping him because I care about him—and, I hope, to keep him from doing the kind of really crazy thing he might do if I weren't helping him. I'm a . . . a stabilizing factor."

That brought a roar of laughter from the violet-eyed man at the wheel.

"Well, what have *you* done to sort this thing out? Broke into Grandpa's boat, tried to steal my briefcase of money, fetched your mother. Maybe your intentions were noble, but you haven't accomplished a damned thing. At least let me try to keep the damage to a minimum."

He glanced over at her then, smiling at her dishevelment. "Okay."

His answer didn't sink in, and she proceeded breathlessly, "Grandpa won't necessarily steal the paintings. He's promised to wait and see what your father does first and—" She stared at him suddenly. "Okay?"

"That's right."

"You won't lock me in the car? You won't turn me in to your father? You won't try and stop me from helping Grandpa?"

He smiled, not showing any teeth, and nodded.

"I'll be damned. That's great! What, well, what are you going to do?"

"Pretend I don't know you."

HE DID, TOO. When they arrived at the house, he said, "I hope we both survive the day. You do, I presume, have a way into the showing?"

She tried not to look too cocky. "I swiped an invitation."

"Naturally."

He climbed out and shut the door as he left her there, sunk down in the seat. No demands to know where Grandpa was at that moment. No questions about their plans. No guesses about when they were going to make their move. It was as if not knowing meant he could pretend that nothing was going to happen, but Sage couldn't quite believe that. Jackson Kirk was no ostrich with his head in the sand.

"He's up to something," she muttered, and gave him five minutes.

A security guard was posted at the gate, which Sage had already cleared by virtue of being in Jackson's car. A second guard was posted at the front entrance to the house, and he merely glanced at her invitation and smiled her in. A cocktail party was starting on the terrace, where Reuben Kirk, elegantly dressed and smiling, was playing the benevolent host. Sage avoided him and ducked out a side door. She didn't even look for Jackson; she didn't want to see him.

Staying among the shrubs and well away from the crowd gathering on the terrace, she headed quickly, stealthily, to a gate down beyond the terrace. She'd noticed it during her previous visits. It was unguarded but, to her dismay, also locked.

"Damn," she whispered. The last thing she wanted to do was to have to pick her first lock—or, worse, help a man in his seventies hoist himself over the six-foot iron fence!

"Such a pessimist." Grandpa's voice came from the bushes beyond the fence. Then he appeared, suave and debonair in a fresh khaki suit. As if he'd been *invited* to the damned showing! Sage kept her disgust to herself as he calmly stuck a key into the simple lock. "You can thank Frances Kirk for helping us over this little hurdle."

"She gave you the key!"

"Swiped it right out of her husband's kitchen."

"Ex-husband. I should have guessed there would be a lock."

"Why? I did and took care of it." He pushed open the gate with a grin of victory, his beady eyes gleaming. "Think you're the only one with a little foresight? I'm not a doddering old man, Sage."

She groaned. "Just come on."

She led him up a grass path toward the terrace, then pushed him behind a clump of trees and insisted he wait there while she surveyed the scene. "I can't believe I actually said that," she muttered. "Survey the scene—good God, what's happening to me?"

"You're having the time of your life," Grandpa said. He lowered his voice. "I see Reuben, but where's your Jackson? He could be more dangerous."

"I don't know and I don't care. I'm sure he has his own plans for today."

Grandpa's thick white eyebrows went up at a sharp angle. "I don't like to come between you two, but I'd just as soon he stay out of my way."

"Don't count on it. I'll be back as soon as I can. *Don't move.*"

He sniffed. "The Killibrews are a bossy lot."

"And none of us likes to take orders."

"An admirable trait, in my opinion."

"Grandpa, you promised me."

He waved off her protest. "You'll find me among the lemons and avocados. Now off you go."

She entered through the front door. The security guard gave her another smile and made no comment on her slight breathlessness. She was sure her hair was sticking out everywhere. She made her way to a bathroom, where she quickly did what she could with it and dabbed on a bit of lipstick. She'd just have to do, in case she bumped into anyone. She hoped she wouldn't.

Chatter and light laughter bubbled in from the terrace as she tiptoed down the hall to the room that had been locked the other day. The paintings had to be there! If not . . . Well, she wouldn't think about that right now. Luck was with her; she was sure of it.

The door was still locked. With a muttered curse Sage rattled the doorknob and would have kicked down the door if it wouldn't have alerted the security guards, the guests and, most particularly, Reuben Kirk.

"This might come in handy."

She jumped and nearly screamed at the sudden sound of Jackson's voice behind her but managed to control herself in time. She started cursing *him* for startling her . . . until she saw the key he held between his fingers.

"Where did you get that?" she asked.

"Filched it."

"Jackson." Her eyes narrowed at him, her heart pounding. Her breasts heaved with each gulp of air. "Jackson, what are you up to?"

He gave her that enigmatic half smile. "Do you want the key or don't you?"

"Of course I do, but I thought you were neutral."

"I am."

"But you're helping me and Grandpa."

"That remains to be seen," he said coolly.

She straightened her shoulders. "Are you sending me into a trap?"

"So suspicious." He picked up her hand, placed the key in her palm and closed her fingers around it. "Go ahead, Sage. Open the door."

Not sure she should, she nonetheless turned around and stuck the key in the lock. It fit. As she pushed open the door and walked into the darkened room, she sensed Jackson following her but didn't hear him so much as breathe. He didn't say a word.

The room was empty.

The floor was bare wood, the walls bare plaster, the windows uncurtained. Not a painting in sight.

Sage whirled around to Jackson. "I've got the wrong room!"

"No, you don't," he replied, leaning against a naked wall. "You're just a day late, that's all."

"What's that supposed to mean?"

"I'm afraid I got here first."

"*What? You . . . you scoundrel!*"

He grinned, unrepentant. "I love it when you call me that."

Then there was a crash behind them, a baseball bat catapulted through a window and Grandpa Killibrew reached an arm in, unlocked the window, pushed it up and climbed inside. He was raving.

"Where are my paintings?" he demanded. "What in hell's going on around here? Sage—"

"Grandpa, I asked you to stay put!"

"Where are my paintings?"

"I *knew* I never should have told you which room I thought they were in!" She groaned in frustration, her fists clenched at her sides. "Grandpa, your paintings aren't here."

"They were," he said.

Her mouth dropped open. "How do you know?"

"Snuck by one night and had a peek, how do you think?"

Before she could say anything, there was a rush of activity behind her, and when she turned, Reuben Kirk was bursting through the door, with Frances not far behind. Jackson's mother shut the door firmly but quietly behind her. Reuben was seething.

"So you've done it," he said, breathing through his nose in an obvious attempt to keep a rein on his anger. "You've stolen the Blue Hill Series."

"I can't steal something that by all rights is mine," Grandpa shot back.

Reuben clenched his fists at his side. "You're an obstinate, impractical, meddlesome old man, Bradford Killibrew. I'm calling the police."

"I wouldn't, Father," Jackson said quietly, stepping forward. "Bradford doesn't have the paintings."

The elder Kirk swung his arms in disgust, fast losing control. "Of course he does! Who the devil else would? He's boasted for months that if I didn't let him buy them back, he'd steal them."

Jackson shook his head, unruffled. "I have them."

Both Reuben and Bradford jumped forward, and Sage herself had to resist going for Jackson's throat.

"I took them yesterday, while you and Mother went sailing," he explained calmly. He seemed unconcerned by his duplicity. "They're safe."

"And you can damn well give them back so I can sell them and get them out of my life forever!" Reuben yelled. "I'm sick of this entire business."

Bradford grunted. "You can sell them back to me, like you promised."

"They're worth ten times what I paid you—at least!"

"As if you need the money."

"As if *you* do! You'd only give it away to one of your causes, and cause some other man grief."

"Ana Luiza didn't leave you because of me," Grandpa spat.

"Are you saying *I* drove her out?"

"She left because of herself, her own needs. You know that as well as I do, but you're too damned stubborn to admit it. Your ego's been damaged."

"This has nothing to do with my 'ego.' I knew the marriage was wrong from the beginning. I was still smarting after Frances's—Oh, never mind, that's all beside the point. Jackson, return my paintings to me at once. I have guests waiting who are anxious to see them."

"Oh, they can see them," Jackson said. "But I don't think they'll want to buy—and I don't think you'll want to sell, Father, once you realize why Bradford's been such a pain in the ass about them."

"Mind your own damned business, Kirk," Bradford grumbled.

Sage looked at Jackson, her curiosity smothering her annoyance. "Jackson, what do you mean?"

He turned to Frances, who stood tensely in front of the door. "Mother?"

She nodded, obviously nervous at her own role in the affair. "You'll have to come upstairs—all of you."

Bradford and Reuben both started to protest, but Sage grabbed her grandfather's wrist and urged him to come along. "Look upon this as Plan E," she told him.

Reuben wasn't about to be the only one left out, and he followed them down the hall and upstairs to the guest room overlooking the pool, where, to Sage's immense surprise, Frances Kirk was staying. She threw open her closet and, with her son's help, pulled out four paintings.

The Blue Hill Series.

Sage gasped, moving slowly toward the seascapes. She'd never seen anything like them. They were exquisite . . . and they were of places she knew. Places she'd played in as a child, explored as a teenager, photographed and loved and remembered as an adult. Places that had always meant something to the Killibrews, and still did.

"Grandpa . . . I . . ." But her throat tightened, and she couldn't speak.

"You didn't look beyond your own anger and pain, Reuben," Frances Kirk said quietly. "And you, Bradford, you should have told him."

"Told me what?" Reuben demanded.

"This series was painted for Bradford's two sons and two granddaughters. They were never meant to be put on the market. The dedications are on the back of the canvases, Reuben, if you'd care to look."

He stared at his ex-wife. "You're saying I've been selfish?"

"No, Reuben, only that you've been turned inward, aware only of your own needs and pain. God knows I understand. I . . . I've been one of the ones to hurt you, perhaps worse than anyone. But you can make this right now. Keep your end of the deal and let Bradford buy back the paintings."

"With what?" he asked scathingly, the impact of this new twist not yet sunk in. "Monopoly money?"

Sage winced, but Grandpa said in a low, proud voice, "I'll get the money."

"No, you won't, dammit, because I have no intention of selling these paintings—to anyone."

"You can't," Sage started to protest, but Jackson grabbed her arm and held her close, urging her to stay out of it. Now wasn't the time to interfere. She had to agree with him.

Reuben Kirk turned to her, his expression showing none of the rage it had held only a moment ago. He seemed strangely placid, in control. This was the Reuben she would want to meet and get to know. "Sage, I'd be delighted if you'd make arrangements to have these four paintings delivered to the people for whom they were intended." He straightened, the polished Academy Award-winning director; for once Sage could see his son in him. "Now if you'll excuse me, I have guests to attend to."

Frances exhaled in relief, tears glistening in her lovely eyes. "Oh, Reuben."

He held up a hand. "Don't, Frances. You're right. I have indulged myself in my own suffering, but don't make it worse. Please. Go—" his voice caught; he cleared his throat before continuing "—go to Bradford, if that's what you want."

"What?" She was truly dumbfounded. "Reuben, what are you talking about? Bradford and I are just friends!"

Grandpa snorted. "Good God, man, are you crazy?"

Reuben looked around at his old friend. "I doubt that very much. You and Frances—Well, it's plain to see. If you two want to be married, I won't make any trouble. There's no point in being miserable just to spare me. I wish you all happiness."

Frances started to speak, but Grandpa cut in first, his tone as serious as Sage had ever heard it. "I had a wife, Reuben, and she died a long time ago. I'll never forget her or look for another. What in blazes would I do with a wife at this stage in my life?"

"You're such an ass, Reuben," Frances said, smiling even as the tears overflowed and coursed down her cheeks. She sniffled. "There's only been one man I've ever loved."

Reuben seemed both embarrassed and relieved, and he fumbled in his pocket for a handkerchief. As Frances took it, he brushed her fingertips with his. "Will you help me explain to my guests?" he asked.

She smiled. "Of course."

They left, and Grandpa shook his head, his mouth twisted. "Those two," he said, then turned to Jackson and Sage. "Well, what about you lovebirds? Shall we take these things downstairs and let Reuben's guests have a look? They've never been shown to the public, you know, and it just might save Reuben some embarrassment if his guests are the first to get a glimpse of the infamous Blue Hill Series."

There was a cockiness to his step as he walked out with one of his paintings that made Sage laugh, and Jackson was grinning, too. She gave him a totally insincere frown. "You're a scoundrel and a sneak, Kirk," she told him, "but I'll deal with you later."

"I certainly hope so."

14

THEY DROVE GRANDPA back to his boat. "If you want the paintings, Grandpa," Sage said as they followed him onto the deck, "by all means take them. You don't have to give them to us until you're ready—if you ever are. You can always change your mind. I won't mention them to the others."

He gave her a curious look. "You won't have to. Didn't you notice the art critic from the L.A. Times at Reuben's little get-together? Now I'd like to know how *he* got in! Reuben swears up and down he wasn't invited. Anyway, the story'll be all over the place by the end of the week." He waved a hand. "No, you go on and take them."

She bit her lip and said tentatively, "Of course, you could present them yourself."

"I don't think so, Sage." He smiled and touched her hair. "Not yet."

Hiding her disappointment, she nodded. Jackson said nothing. This was between her and her grandfather. Between Killibrews. She appreciated his understanding, and yet she wished he could explain her grandfather to her. There was so much of Bradford Killibrew she didn't understand, so much that remained a mystery to her.

"Oh, one more thing." As spry as ever, Grandpa ducked below, emerging in a minute with a carefully covered canvas. "This is for your Auntie Killibrew." He grinned wickedly. "Wouldn't want the old battle-ax to feel left out."

He showed them the painting, a stunning view from the bay in Maine on which Auntie's cottage was set, with the unique touches that Sage was beginning to recognize as her grandfather's. "She'll be amazed," Sage said.

"She'll be furious," Grandpa said with a grunt. "I was right out in her damned bay without her ever knowing it. She'll wonder why I didn't pop over for tea."

Sage had to smile. "And why didn't you?"

"Because I'd have been tempted to stay. Killibrew Traders was in trouble, your uncle was trying to revive Summerfield Shoe.... Timing just wasn't right."

"I'm hoping it will be someday."

"Maybe next summer, you never know. I figure stewing about me spying on her will keep your Auntie alive another winter, and me, well, I'm moseying on down to Mexico, seeing some friends, trying some new techniques. The North Atlantic in summer, though, is hard to beat."

Sage kissed him on his leathery cheek. "So are you, Grandpa."

He hugged her then, patting her back as he held her. "You give them all the paintings," he said, his voice choked, "and tell them . . . tell them whether or not I'm there with you, all of you are on my mind, always."

"I love you, Grandpa."

"And I love you."

To her relief Jackson didn't say a word until they were back at his house and he had two glasses of wine poured. They sat out on the terrace. Sage's hands were shaking, and she wanted to cry. Everything seemed finished. And yet, in a certain way, nothing seemed finished. She wasn't ready to pack up and head home to Colorado; it didn't seem right.

"He's not lonely," she said more to herself than to Jackson. "I know he's not lonely."

Jackson smiled with an empathy that made her heart stop. Lord, she thought, how could she leave this man? How could she just go back to her life in Colorado and pretend none of what had happened this past week had touched her soul?

It was simple. She couldn't.

"Your grandfather is doing exactly what he wants to do," Jackson said, "maybe even what he has to do. Don't feel sorry for him, Sage."

"I'm not. I guess I'm just feeling sorry for myself, and for Juniper and Summerfield and my father. Especially them because they haven't seen him. It's like . . . it's like they don't even know him."

"That's what the paintings are for. They're his way of telling them who he is, what he's become."

She nodded. "I know, and I guess I just have to respect that."

"Sage..." Jackson leaned forward, his forearms on his knees, his eyes vibrant and glittering in the waning evening sun. "I don't think it's you or your family that Bradford's avoiding right now. I think it's New Hampshire that unnerves him. Going back there, being among people who knew him as a wily Yankee businessman in a gray flannel suit, being back with his old life—and old memories."

"My grandmother."

"He doesn't want to forget her, not at all. I think he prefers to remember her and his old life from a comfortable distance. New Hampshire dredges up the memories in the wrong way for him. But—" a gleam came into his eyes "—but he never said *you* couldn't go see *him*."

It took awhile for what he was saying to sink in, and when it did, Sage didn't know whether she wanted to jump up and laugh or throw up her arms in confusion. Finally she said, "No, he didn't. But could you see his face if we all showed up in Mexico? I mean, he'd have a fit!"

Jackson shrugged. "He likes trouble; keeps him going."

"I do believe you're right." She laughed, clapping her hands together as a new plot began to form. "A family reunion in Mexico, say, at Christmas. We wouldn't tell Grandpa ahead of time, of course; otherwise, he just might take off for Brazil or someplace. He'll kill me, you know."

"He'd love it."

"You think so?" She was already beginning to think so herself.

"Sure."

She grinned. "Christmas it is, then."

Jackson stared down at his glass of wine. "And what will you do between now and then?"

There was an uncertainty in his voice that she hadn't heard before, and when she looked at him, the wine and contentment warming her, she saw he wasn't smiling. And she knew what he was asking. It was simple enough: where were they going from here? She wondered if he had ideas of his own, and something told her he did. He was Jackson Kirk, after all, a schemer just like she was . . . and the man she couldn't imagine her life without.

"I don't know," she said, trying to keep her voice steady, "but then I never do until I'm actually doing it. I—" she shrugged with a self-consciousness that was both surprising and unwelcome "—I don't live a regular existence."

"Meaning you have no plans."

"I guess that's what I mean. I've always managed to find something to keep me occupied and solvent, but I don't spend a whole lot of time planning and worrying about it." She sipped some wine, her heart thudding. "You?"

"I have a project," he announced calmly, leaning back.

She finished off her wine and nodded. Maybe she'd misunderstood what he was asking, read into it more than was there. Maybe she was hearing uncertainty and seeing longing when all the man wanted was to know whether or not she was going to be a pest. Oh, hell, she thought, I'm acting like a complete ninny! *Ask* the man what's on his mind!

But she couldn't, not yet. Instead, she said, "Oh. Well, of course. I understand."

Something flickered in his eyes. Amusement? No, there was nothing the least bit amusing about what she'd said or, certainly, about what she was thinking. He'd be a cad if he were amused. "Would you like to hear about it?"

She shrugged her shoulders. "Okay."

The flicker deepened into a half smile—a *knowing* half smile that reminded Sage of the man who'd burst into the Happy Trails Lounge knowing more about Bradford Killibrew and her briefcase full of money than she did. This, she thought, was her rogue. Her love.

"The project begins with a trip to Portsmouth, New Hampshire, to deliver some paintings and meet and interview Juniper Killibrew and her husband, Calvin Gilliam, Summerfield Killibrew and 'Auntie' Killibrew, who seems to have no verifiable first name. Then on to the South Pacific to deliver a painting to Mr. and Dr. Killibrew, on whom I have virtually no information, and to meet and interview them. While I'm at it, I thought I'd visit my friend who studies ants. After that it's on to Mexico to do the first interview ever with the reclusive artist Bradford Killibrew. That should be . . . oh, around Christmas, I should think. What do you think?"

It had been all she could do to keep her cool. "Kirk, are you making this up?"

"Who, me?"

"Kirk . . ."

"I have major funding to do a documentary on Bradford Killibrew from the Corporation for Public Broadcasting. People are talking about your grandfather being the next Andrew Wyeth, you know."

"Has he agreed to this?"

"Only because he wants a new boat. He figures the 'notoriety,' as he calls it, will up the prices of his paintings and he can get his boat. Plus, of course, he has his causes to support."

"Unbelievable. But I, um, noticed there's no trip to Colorado in the works."

"I'm hoping I won't need one."

"Oh."

His mouth twitched. "Don't say 'oh' like you know what I'm talking about, Sage Killibrew, because you don't. Don't be a paranoid simp, dammit. I need a partner on this documentary. You said you wanted to do more with your photography, maybe get into this sort of thing. I was hoping you'd consider teaming up with me."

Her eyebrows went up. "Was?"

"What a pain in the rear you are." There was nothing but affection in his tone. "Am, then. I *am* hoping you'll consider."

"I have strong opinions."

"An asset; so do I."

"We'll probably argue."

"And make up when we're through."

"Are you *sure* you're not making up this documentary stuff?"

"I'll show you the contract."

"Never mind, I believe you."

His eyes caught hers. "Do you?"

She smiled. "Yes . . . always."

HE'D LIED, of course. The contract wasn't in hand, just on the way but that was a "mere stretching of the facts for my own convenience," he'd put it. The short wait allowed them time to make a quick trip to Colorado, where Sage showed him her land. They'd pitched a tent and slept together in one sleeping bag, the better, she had insisted, to combat the cold. Jackson hadn't argued. Sage also introduced him to her friends. Diana said she herself couldn't have conjured up a more perfect man for Sage. They explained their plans for the coming months, and everyone was supportive and enthusiastic.

Then it was back to Coronado. The contract had arrived, and they finalized plans, alerted Jackson's small team and discussed possibilities for the documentary over dinner with Reuben Kirk. Frances Kirk was there, too, and they appeared rooted in La Jolla, she in no hurry to return to San Francisco, or he to Brazil. As Frances put it, if they ever finished talking, they might get back to work and maybe do some traveling.

Sage had the feeling they were doing lots more than just talking, and she couldn't help smiling. She loved a happy ending.

After that they went to work. Sage supposed she surprised Jackson with her capacity for long hours and her zest for perfection as much as he did her with his. They were impulsive and adventurous, perhaps, but not lazy. And to her relief their similar temperaments, rather than being a constant source of tension, proved a stabilizing factor during times of disagreement and fatigue so bone-deep it made them irrational. If they weren't alike, she'd decided, they wouldn't be able to stand each other. There was so much energy between them, so much excitement and craziness, that she sometimes wondered if they'd wear themselves out before they turned forty. And yet every morning Sage awoke filled with ideas, eager for the new day.

The only problem was that each new day never included lovemaking. Since California they'd been more like buddies than lovers. Professionals who refused to mix business and pleasure.

Monks, she thought with frustration as she spread a blanket on a secluded private beach, owned by a friend of Reuben's, in Hawaii. It was eight weeks since they'd left California, eight weeks since they'd been alone together, eight weeks since they'd made love. They were between visits to her parents and Jackson's ant researcher, and without arguing, virtually without words, they'd chosen this beach, this morning, this perfect spot on the sand. They sat down together. It was a magnificent day, the sky and water both blue and clear, the air warm but not oppressive. Sage could feel her body begin to relax as she slid over to the edge of the blanket and

worked her feet into the white sand. And she could feel
herself begin to grow as liquid as the sea, pulsating with
the same rhythm as the waves slapping the shore, as she
studied Jackson's browned torso and felt the familiar
need.

As far as she was concerned, he was as sexy now as the
first moment she'd seen him, emerging from the depths
of her imagination. Her need for him hadn't dissipated
during the weeks of work and celibacy. It was there, a
constant, always gnawing at her mind, her senses, her
soul. She would have gone for him as boldly as she had
in California; she wasn't waiting for him to make the first
move. But it hadn't seemed right. Never mind that they'd
lacked the necessary privacy during most of the past
weeks. Even when they could have snuck off for a few
hours alone or could have arranged to spend entire nights
together, they hadn't. Without discussing the reasons
Sage had gone along with the unspoken agreement . . . had, in fact, in some ways promoted their celibacy. Everything had happened so fast in San Diego and
sex had been such a compulsive, motivating force between them that now they needed—*she* needed—to
know there was more to their relationship. She wanted
to know she loved Jackson Kirk for himself.

And she did. In bed with him or out, she liked him,
wanted him, loved him. Falling for him in San Diego
hadn't been just an impulsive act; it had been real.

Jackson rolled onto his back, then over onto his stomach, propping himself on his elbows as he looked up at
her. Her knees were almost at her breasts, her feet covered in sand up to her ankles, and she wore a simple tank
suit. Something about his look—the intensity of it, the
frank way it probed her—made her breasts swell with an

aching desire, and she was almost embarrassed when her nipples grew erect under the thin fabric. He would notice, of course.

Yet he made no comment about the obvious state of her body. Instead, he said very seriously, "There's something I need to tell you."

"Sure. What's up?" She tried to sound nonchalant, a friend to whom he could tell anything. Of course she wanted to be much more than a friend.

He dug his toes into the sand at the lower edge of the blanket, and she noticed that every muscle in his lightly tanned legs was tensed. He wore a bikini swimsuit. Dark blue and very sexy. She wondered if she should tell him so. The gravity of his expression, however, dissuaded her. The man clearly had something on his mind.

Then he said, almost abruptly, "Sage, I'm sorry, but I can't go on like this."

It wasn't what she expected. Not what she wanted to hear. Her head spun, and a hot knife seemed to slice through her. Had she been presumptuous? Had she misread everything during the past eight weeks? Good God, what was the man talking about!

Ask him, her inner voice said. Sitting very still, she asked in as even a voice as she could muster, "What do you mean?"

"I mean everything. You, me, the way we've been living."

She said nothing, mostly because she didn't know what to say, didn't know what he meant.

He looked away from her, straight ahead at the water, and she felt his sigh more than heard it. "We'll never lead an ordinary life, you and I. That's pretty obvious. We both have so much energy, so many ideas. We've enough projects in mind to last a lifetime."

"I thought that was good," she said, hearing the breathlessness, the confusion and terror, in her voice. What was he leading up to?

He gave a curt nod; or maybe it wasn't a nod at all but just an indication that he'd heard her—or not even that. Maybe he was just warding off an insect.

"Jackson?" she prodded.

"I love to travel, you know that, and I don't want to—couldn't—give it up. But I also need a base, some roots, some sense of balance in my life. I'm not talking about settling down in the conventional sense. Not altogether, at least." He exhaled, his own frustration showing. "I was thinking more in terms of planning expeditions, not just jumping at projects, perhaps even limiting them to certain months of the year. It would mean being less impulsive, less spontaneous."

"I see," she said stiffly. Actually, she didn't. "Are we talking about some kind of career crisis here?"

"What?" He glanced up at her as if she had missed the point entirely and might be a little daft. "Career crisis? What the hell are you talking about?"

She was getting downright irritated. "I am trying to figure out what *you're* talking about! Here we are, alone for the first time in weeks, and you're telling me you want to change the way you make your living. Okay, fine. I don't mind listening. I'll even offer advice, if that's what you want. But, Lord—I mean, really, Jackson, I thought . . ." She threw up her hands.

He frowned at her, his eyes glittering in the Hawaiian sun. "You thought what?"

She huffed and refused to look at him. "Frankly, I thought we could talk about us."

"Ass," he said affectionately, and when she shot him a look, she saw he was grinning. "That *is* what I'm talking about."

"You could have fooled me," she muttered.

"Do *you* want to continue as we've been doing for the past two months?"

"No."

"Have you thought about why?"

She glared at him, but the glint in his eye made her smile. "You're being obtuse, Kirk."

"And you're not answering my question. Have you thought about why you don't want to go on like this?"

"Well, for one thing—" She broke off, staring at the ocean in front of her. The tide was rolling in, bringing with it a soft, fragrant breeze. "For one thing, we don't get much time alone."

"Minor."

"*Minor!*" She whipped around in a surprised rage. "Well, it's not minor to me, dammit! As I assumed you discovered in California, I'm not exactly a nun. I mean, it's nice to be alone with you just to talk, but I—Oh, never mind."

"No, say it."

She could swear he was holding back a grin but couldn't be sure. Tucking a lock of hair behind her ear, she frowned down at him. "You're going to insist, aren't you?"

"Mmm."

"Okay, Kirk. I'd like us to make love once in a while. So there."

He was laughing softly, and when Sage whirled around to tackle him, she saw the light and warmth and roguishness in his violet eyes. "Scoundrel," she muttered and threw herself on him, going for his elbows to knock him off balance. He fell over onto his back, but one arm crooked around her waist and brought her with him. Somehow she ended up on top, lying lengthwise on him, feeling the tantalizing firmness and warmth of his body beneath her. Her reaction was as instant as it was intense, and she felt herself melting, quaking, aching with arousal.

The arm that had dragged her into such a precarious position settled low across her back, and the hand slipped down and patted her sleek upper thigh. Her breasts seemed ready to burst out of her swimsuit as they pressed against the solid muscles of his chest.

"I meant minor," he said, reaching up with his other hand to pull a lock of hair from her mouth as she lifted her torso off him, "in the sense of a minor problem."

She scowled, not in the least angry. "You could have said so."

"I didn't think I needed to. Have the last eight weeks made you paranoid?"

"No, they've made me, well, deprived of a certain level of physical satisfaction."

He laughed. "That's about as polite a way of saying it as I've ever heard. What you're indicating—" his eyes dropped to her breasts, their nipples thrust out against the nylon suit "—in more than just words is that you can't possibly have a serious discussion about our lives and where we go from here until we've made love?"

She could feel his own "indication" pressing against her and knew she wasn't the only one who wanted to postpone talk. She said devilishly, "Well, not necessarily. If you want to talk first—"

"Not likely," he said in a voice gravelly with desire, and he pulled her down against him, his mouth seeking hers. His tongue plunged immediately into her mouth, met hers, and the yearning that filled them both flowed from one to the other. The kiss was long and luxurious, probing and wet, pulsing. Sage was breathless when it ended. But that didn't matter.

"How I resisted touching you . . ." Jackson murmured, still in that low, gravelly voice.

He eased the shoulder straps of her suit down her arms, slowly lower, until her breasts were revealed to his gaze and the breeze and the warm sun. Holding her by the waist, he lifted her higher against him, then brought her gently down, taking one breast in his mouth, licking all around it with the wet heat of his tongue, then stiffening his tongue and flicking it against her nipple . . . until finally she moaned aloud.

"Jackson . . . don't stop . . ."

He didn't. But as he took her other breast into his mouth, repeating his sensual caresses, he slid the rest of her bathing suit down to her hips. She thought it would be cast off into the sand in seconds, but instead, he thrust his hands inside the suit and grabbed her buttocks, pushing them hard against his own wild arousal.

"I don't think I can wait," he breathed, pulling his mouth from her breast and looking up at her with desire and too many other emotions for her to even begin to sort out.

"Mmm, it's been too long . . . far too long."

She took charge, rolling off him for a few seconds to quickly dispose of her suit, and then climbed on top of him.

"Far too long," he agreed. He groaned as he entered her. Loving the feel of him inside her, Sage stayed still, savoring their closeness for a moment before beginning to move rhythmically. The tide had edged up and lapped at them, but they ignored it, pulsing with a rhythm more rapid, perhaps even more powerful than the tide itself.

They lay together afterward, sated, letting the waves roll onto their hot, naked bodies as the pulsing inside them slowed to match the gentle undulating of the sea itself. Sage had never felt so full, so at peace.

After a long while, after they'd put their suits back on and pulled the blanket higher onto the beach and gone for a swim, they opened up the picnic basket. Sage was ravenous. "Now," she said to Jackson, passing him a sandwich, "what's this about leading a less impulsive, less spontaneous life?"

"Wipe that cocky grin off your face, Killibrew," he warned, teasing. "I will *try* to be less 'obtuse.'"

Her grin only broadened. "Please do."

"What I was trying to say in a roundabout sort of way is that I love you."

"Really? That's a heck of a way—"

"*Sage!*"

"I'm sorry. Really, I am."

"But you don't believe me."

"Of course I believe you. I'm just not sure what 'I love you' means to you."

He smiled. "Didn't the last hour or so give you the slightest idea?"

"Well, yes, but..." She sighed and unwrapped her sandwich to give herself something to do while she considered what she was about to say. Then she thought, *what* am *I about to say?* "I guess I mean in practical terms."

"Practical terms... This from the lady who waltzed into a seedy San Diego bar with a suitcase full of money?"

"Monopoly money," she corrected. "Okay, suppose we resume making love every moment we can. I've enjoyed getting to know you on a different level the past two months, and I admit I *like* you as well as love you, but what about the future? So far you've been providing protection during our lovemaking, but what if we decide to stop? What if we decide we want a *child*, Jackson?"

"A child," he repeated.

"Yes, haven't you thought about children?"

He was staring at her.

"I mean, not *tomorrow*, for heaven's sake, but down the road what if that's what we decide. Well, I don't know about you, but I don't want to have an illegitimate child. It's just not my style. I know I'm impulsive and all that, but where certain things are concerned, I like being conventional. So even though I'm madly in love with you and can't imagine life without you..." She shrugged, leaving it at that.

"Sage."

She couldn't look at him. Did he understand what she was saying? Did *she*?

"Sage," he went on, "what the hell do you think I was trying to say earlier? A hit-or-miss life with you isn't enough. I want more. God knows we'll never be hopelessly conventional and we'll always have that urge to be spontaneous. That's good. It's who we are. But I don't want to just 'wing it' with you, Sage. I want us to be us forever."

She smiled over at him, brimming with emotion. "So do I."

"A promise on a Hawaiian beach isn't enough for me."

"I don't understand."

He leaned toward her, his violet eyes picking up the light and the colors of the sunset. "I'd like you to consider marrying me, Sage."

"I don't have to consider it. Of *course* I'll marry you, Jackson!"

But he was shaking his head. "No, this can't be an impulsive decision on your part. I've been thinking about marriage since Coronado—frankly, since I caught you under the bougainvillea at my father's."

"I am *not* being impulsive! I love you, dammit, and I want to marry you. I—" But he'd gotten that determined Kirk look on his face, and she knew arguing was pointless. "You won't take yes for an answer, will you?"

"Not until Mexico."

"*Mexico!* Jackson, my family will be there, and Grandpa and—My God, even Auntie Killibrew's coming! No, I'll give you my yes tonight."

He shook his head, adamant.

She opened her mouth to argue, but a sudden mad idea popped into her head, and instead, she shrugged. "Okay, you win. Mexico it is."

"Sage?" He peered at her. "Sage, are you up to something?"

She laughed and started on her sandwich. "Ahh, I do love you, Jackson Kirk."

URGENT!! URGENT!! URGENT!! URGENT!!

TO: BRADFORD KILLIBREW
    ACAPULCO, MEXICO

GRANDPA: NEED YOUR HELP. NOWHERE ELSE
TO TURN. WILL ARRIVE ACAPULCO
CHRISTMAS EVE WITH MAN I LOVE. HAVE NEW
BOAT READY FOR WEDDING. PREPARE MENU
AND INVITE GUESTS. WILL SEE YOU THERE.
REPEAT: URGENT.

SAGE KILLIBREW

URGENT!! URGENT!! URGENT!! URGENT!!

TO: JUNIPER KILLIBREW GILLIAM
    SUMMERFIELD HOUSE
    PORTSMOUTH, NH USA

JUNIPER: NEED YOUR HELP. NOWHERE ELSE
TO TURN. SISTER SAGE AT IT AGAIN. INTENDS
TO MARRY SCOUNDREL JACKSON KIRK. NO
NEED TO STOP HER; HE'S JUST HER TYPE.
BRING FAMILY AND MONEY TO COVER
WEDDING EXPENSES ABOARD MY BOAT IN
ACAPULCO CHRISTMAS DAY. INFORMAL
DRESS. WE'RE HAVING TACOS AND DOS
EQUIS BEER. WILL SEE YOU THERE.
REPEAT: URGENT.

GRANDPA KILLIBREW

Harlequin Temptation

COMING NEXT MONTH

#193 SPIRIT OF LOVE JoAnn Ross

When a handsome stranger tried to convince Justine that he'd been dreaming of her for months, she was highly skeptical. But the more she saw of Colin, the easier it was to picture herself haunting him in the wee hours....

#194 THE NESTING INSTINCT Corey Keator

Grey Powell might have outbid Megan Sinclair on the house she desperately wanted, but the heirloom hidden inside would be hers! Much to her surprise, Grey willingly gave her access to the house ... and anything else she cared to explore.

#195 MORE THAN WORDS Elizabeth Glenn

Lee Ann Chung was at her wits' end with her hopelessly unruly dog, Doofus, so she enrolled him in obedience school. There she met the star canine, but it was his master who exuded a rare brand of animal magnetism....

#196 OVER THE RAINBOW Sandra Lee

After a storm brought Hal into Dana's life, she thought clear skies were finally coming her way. But dreaming of a future with him, she realized, was like chasing rainbows....

PAMELA BROWNING

...is fireworks on the green at the Fourth of July and prayers said around the Thanksgiving table. It is the dream of freedom realized in thousands of small towns across this great nation.

But mostly, the Heartland is its people. People who care about and help one another. People who cherish traditional values and give to their children the greatest gift, the gift of love.

American Romance presents HEARTLAND, an emotional trilogy about people whose memories, hopes and dreams are bound up in the acres they farm.

HEARTLAND...the story of America.

Don't miss these heartfelt stories: American Romance #237 SIMPLE GIFTS (March), #241 FLY AWAY (April), and #245 HARVEST HOME (May).

HRT-1